# The Investment of Influence

## Newell Dwight Hillis

# Contents

# THE INVESTMENT
# OF INFLUENCE

BY

Newell Dwight Hillis

## DEDICATION

**M**any years have now passed since we first met. During all this time you have been an unfailing guide and helper. Your friendship has doubled life's joys and halved its sorrows. You have strengthened me where I was weak and weakened me where I was too strong. You have borne my burdens and lent me strength to bear my own.

Because I have learned from you in example, what I here teach in precept, I dedicate this book

TO YOU
 --whether toiling in field or forum,
in home or market place,

TO YOU--MY FRIEND

## FOREWORD.

The glory of our fathers was their emphasis of the principle of self-care and self-culture. Finding that he who first made the most of himself was best fitted to make something of others, the teachers of yesterday unceasingly plied men with motives of personal responsibility. Influenced by the former generation, our age has organized the principle of individualism into its home, its school, its market-place and forum. By reason of the increase in gold, books, travel and personal luxuries, some now feel that selfness is beginning to degenerate into selfishness. The time, therefore, seems to have fully come when the principle of self-care should receive its complement through the principle of care for others. These chapters assert the debt of wealth to poverty, the debt of wisdom to ignorance, the debt of strength to weakness. If "A Man's Value to Society" affirms the duty of self-culture and character, these studies emphasize the law of social sympathy and social service.

Newell Dwight Hillis.

## INFLUENCE, AND THE ATMOSPHERE
## MAN CARRIES.

I do not believe the world is dying for new ideas. A teacher has a high place amongst us, but someone is wanted here and abroad far more than a teacher. It is power we need, power that shall help us to solve our practical problems, power that shall help us to realize a high, individual, spiritual life, power that shall make us daring enough to act out all we have seen in vision, all we have learnt in principle from Jesus Christ."-- *Charles A. Berry*.

"And Saul sent messengers to take David: and when they saw the company of prophets prophesying, and Samuel standing as appointed over them, the Spirit of God was upon the messengers of Saul, and they also prophesied. And when it was told Saul, he sent other messengers and they prophesied likewise. And Saul sent messengers again the third time, and they prophesied also. Then went Saul to Ramah, and he said, Where are Samuel and David? And one said, Behold they be at Naioth. And Saul went thither, and the Spirit of God came on him also and he prophesied. Wherefore man said: Is Saul also among the prophets?"--*I. Samuel, xix, 20-21*.

Nature's forces carry their atmosphere. The sun gushes forth light unquenchable; coals throw off heat; violets are larger in influence than bulb; pomegranates and spices crowd the house with sweet odors. Man also has his atmosphere. He is a force-bearer and a force-producer. He journeys forward, exhaling influences. Scientists speak of the magnetic circle. Artists express the same idea by the halo of light emanating from the divine head. Business men understand this principle, those skilled in promoting great enterprises bring the men to be impressed into a room and create an atmosphere around them. In measuring Kossuth's influence over the multitudes that thronged and pressed upon him the historian said: "We must first reckon with the orator's physical bulk and then carry the measuring-line about his atmosphere."

Thinking of the evil emanating from a bad man, Bunyan made Apollyon's nostrils emit flames. Edward Everett insists that Daniel Webster's eyes during his greatest speech literally emitted sparks. Had we tests fine enough we would doubtless find each man's personality the center of outreaching influences. He himself may be utterly unconscious of this exhalation of moral forces, as he is of the contagion of disease from his body. But if light is in him he shines; if darkness rules he shades, if his heart glows with love he warms; if frozen with selfishness he chills; if corrupt he poisons; if pure-hearted he cleanses. We watch with wonder the apparent flight of the sun through space, glowing upon dead planets, shortening winter and bringing summer, with birds, leaves and fruits. But that is not half so wonderful as the passage of a human heart, glowing and sparkling with ten thousand effects, as it moves through life. The soul, like the sun, has its atmosphere, and is over against its fellows, for light, warmth and transformation.

All great writers have had their incident of the atmosphere their hero carried. Centuries ago King Saul sent his officers to arrest a seer who had publicly indicted the tyrant for outbreaking sins. When the soldier entered the prophet's presence he was so profoundly affected by the majesty of his character that he forgot the commission and his lord's command, asking rather to become the good man's protector. Likewise with the second group of soldiers--coming to arrest, they remained to befriend. Then the King's anger was exceedingly hot against him who had become a conscience for the throne. Rushing forth from his palace, like an angry lion from his lair, the King sought the place where this man of God was teaching the people. But, lo! when the King entered the brave man's presence his courage, fidelity and integrity overcame Saul and conquered him unto confession of his wickedness. Just here we may remember that stout-hearted Pilate, with a legion of mailed soldiers to protect him, trembled and quaked before his silent prisoner. And King Agrippa on his throne was afraid, when Paul lifting his chains, fronted him with words of righteousness and judgment. Carlyle says that in 1848, during the riot in Paris, the mob swept down a street blazing with cannon, killed the soldiers, spiked the guns, only to be stopped a few blocks beyond by an old, white-haired man who uncovered and signaled for silence. Then the leader of the mob said: "Citizens, it is De la Eure. Sixty years of pure life is about to address you!" A true man's presence transformed a mob that cannon could not conquer.

Montaigne's illustration of atmosphere was Julius Caesar. When the great Roman was still a youth, he was captured by pirates and chained to the oars as a galley-slave; but Caesar told stories, sang songs, declaimed with endless good humor. Chains bound Caesar to the oars, and his words bound the pirates to himself. That night he supped with the captain. The second day his knowledge of currents, coasts and the route of treasure-ships made him first mate; then he won the sailors over, put the captain in irons, and ruled the ship like a king; soon after, he sailed the ship as a prize into a Roman port. If this incident is credible, a youth who in four days can talk the chains off his wrists, talk himself into the captaincy, talk a pirate ship into his own hands as booty, is not to be accounted for by his eloquent words. His speech was but a tithe of his power, and wrought its spell only when personality had first created a sympathetic atmosphere. Only a fraction of a great man's character can manifest itself in speech; for the character is inexpressibly finer and larger than his words. The narrative of Washington's exploits is the smallest part of his work. Sheer weight of personality alone can account for him. Happy the man of moral energy all compact, whose mere presence, like that of Samuel, the seer, restrains others, softens and transforms them. This is a thing to be written on a man's tomb: "***His presence made bad men good.***"

This mysterious bundle of forces called man, moving through society, exhaling blessings or blightings, gets its meaning from the capacity of others to receive its influences. Man is not so wonderful in his power to mold other lives, as in his readiness to be molded. Steel to hold, he is wax to take. The Daguerrean plate and the Aeolian harp do but meagerly interpret his receptivity. Therefore, some philosophers think character is but the sum total of those many-shaped influences called climate, food, friends, books, industries. As a lump of clay is lifted to the wheel by the potter's hand, and under gentle pressure takes on the lines of a beautiful cup or vase, so man sets forth a mere mass of mind; soon, under the gentle touch of love, hope, ambition, he stands forth in the aspect of a Cromwell, a Milton or a Lincoln.

Standing at the center of the universe, a thousand forces come rushing in to report themselves to the sensitive soul-center. There is a nerve in man that runs out to every room and realm in the universe. Only a tithe of the world's truth and beauty finds access to the lion or lark; they look out as one in castle tower whose only window is a slit in the rock. But man dwells in a glass dome; to him the world lies open on every side. Every fact and force outside has a desk inside man where it makes up its reports. The ear reports all sounds and songs; the eye all sights and scenes; the reason all arguments, judgment each "ought" and "ought not," the religious faculty reports messages coming from a foreign clime.

Man's mechanism stands at the center of the universe with telegraph-lines extending in every direction. It is a marvelous pilgrimage he is making through life while myriad influences stream in upon him. It is no small thing to carry such a mind for three-score years under the glory of the heavens, through the glory of the earth, midst the majesty of the summer and the sanctity of the winter, while all things animate and inanimate rush in through open windows. For one thus sensitively constituted every moment trembles with possibilities; every hour is big with destiny. The neglected blow cannot afterward be struck on the cold iron; once the stamp is given to the soft metal it cannot be effaced. Well did Ruskin say; "Take your vase of Venice glass out of the furnace and strew chaff over it in its transparent heat, and recover that to its clearness and rubied glory when the north wind has blown upon it; but do not think to strew chaff over the child fresh from God's presence and to bring the heavenly colors back to him--at least in this world." We are accountable to God for our influence; this it is "that gives us pause."

Gentle as is the atmosphere about us, it presses with a weight of fourteen pounds to the square inch. No infant's hand feels its weight; no leaf of aspen or wing of bird detects this heavy pressure, for the fluid air presses equally in all directions. Just so gentle, yet powerful, is the moral atmosphere of a good man as it presses upon and shapes his kind. He who hath made man in his own image hath endowed him with this forceful presence. Ten-talent men, eminent in knowledge and refinement, eminent in art and wealth, do, indeed, illustrate this. Proof also comes from obscurity, as pearls from homely oyster shells. Working among the poor of London, an English author searched out the life-career of an apple woman. Her history makes the story of kings and queens contemptible. Events had appointed her to poverty, hunger, cold and two rooms in a tenement. But there were three orphan boys sleeping in an ash-box whose lot was harder. She dedicated her heart and life to the little waifs. During two and forty years she mothered and reared some twenty orphans--gave them home and bed and food; taught them all she knew; helped some to obtain a scant knowledge of the trades; helped others off to Canada and America. The author says she had misshapen features, but that an exquisite smile was on the dead face. It must have been so. She "had a beautiful soul," as Emerson said of Longfellow. Poverty disfigured the apple woman's garret, and want made it wretched, nevertheless, God's most beautiful angels hovered over it. Her life was a blossom event in London's history. Social reform has felt her influence. Like a broken vase the perfume of her being will sweeten literature and society a thousand years after we are gone.

The Greek poet says men knew when the goddess came to Thebes because of the blessings she left in her track. Her footprints were not in the sea, soon obliterated, nor in the snow, quickly melting, but in fields and forests. This unseen friend, passing by the tree blackened by a thunderbolt, stayed her step; lo! the woodbine sprang up and covered the tree's nakedness. She lingered by the stagnant pool--the pool became a flowing spring. She rested upon a fallen log--from decay and death came moss, the snowdrop and the anemone. At the crossing of the brook were her footprints; not in mud downward, but in violets that sprang up in her pathway. O beautiful prophecy! literally fulfilled 2,000 years afterward in the life of the London apple woman, whose atmosphere sweetened bitter hearts and made evil into good.

Wealth and eminent position witness not less powerfully the transforming influence of exalted characters. "My lords," said Salisbury, "the reforms of this century have been chiefly due to the presence here of one man--Lord Shaftesbury. The genius of his life was expressed when last he addressed you. He said: 'When I feel age creeping upon me I am deeply grieved, for I cannot bear to go away and leave the world with so much misery in it.'" So long as Shaftesbury lived, England beheld a standing rebuke of all wrong and injustice. How many iniquities shriveled up in his presence! This man, representing the noblest ancestry, wealth and culture, wrought numberless reforms. He became a voice for the poor and weak. He gave his life to reform acts and corn laws; he emancipated the enslaved boys and girls toiling in mines and factories; he exposed and made impossible the horrors of that inferno in which chimney-sweeps live; he founded twoscore industrial,

ragged and trade schools; he established shelters for the homeless poor; when Parliament closed its sessions at midnight Lord Shaftesbury went forth to search out
poor prodigals sleeping under Waterloo or Blackfriars bridge, and often in a single
night brought a score to his shelter. When the funeral cortege passed through Pall
Mall and Trafalgar square on its way to Westminster Abbey, the streets for a mile
and a half were packed with innumerable thousands. The costermongers lifted a
large banner on which were inscribed these words: "I was sick and in prison and ye
visited me." The boys from the ragged schools lifted these words; "I was hungry and
naked and ye fed me." All England felt the force of that colossal character. To-day
at that central point in Piccadilly where the highways meet and thronging multitudes go surging by, the English people have erected the statue of Shaftesbury--the
fitting motto therefor; "The reforms of this century have been chiefly due to the
presence and influence of Shaftesbury." If our generation is indeed held back from
injustice and anarchy and bloodshed, it will be because Shaftesbury the peer, and
Samuel, the seer, are duplicated in the lives of our great men, who stand forth to
plead the cause of the poor and weak.

But man's atmosphere is equally potent to blight and to shrivel. Not time, but
man, is the great destroyer. History is full of the ruins of cities and empires. "Innumerable Paradises have come and gone; Adams and Eves many," happy one day,
have been "miserable exiles" the next; and always because some satanic ambition or
passion or person entering has cast baneful shadow o'er the scene. Men talk of the
scythe of time and the tooth of time. But, said the art historian: "Time is scythe-
less and toothless; it is we who gnaw like the worm; we who smite like the scythe.
Fancy what treasures would be ours to-day if the delicate statues and temples of the
Greeks, if the broad roads and massy walls of the Romans, if the noble architecture,
castles and towns of the Middle Ages had not been ground to dust by blind rage of
man. It is man that is the consumer; he is moth and mildew and flame." All the
galleries and temples and libraries and cities have been destroyed by his baneful
presence. Thrice armies have made an arsenal of the Acropolis; ground the precious marbles to powder, and mixed their dust with his ashes. It was man's ax and
hammer that dashed down the carved work of cathedrals and turned the treasure
cities into battle-fields, and opened galleries to the mold of sea winds. Disobedience
to law has made cities a heap and walled cities ruins. Man is the pestilence that

walketh in darkness. Man is the destruction that wasteth at noonday.

When Mephistopheles appears in human form his presence falls upon homes like the black pall of the consuming plague, that robes cities for death. The classic writer tells of an Indian princess sent as a present to Alexander the Great. She was lovely as the dawn; yet what especially distinguished her was a certain rich perfume in her breath; richer than a garden of Persian roses. A sage physician discovered her terrible secret. This lovely woman had been reared upon poisons from infancy until she herself was the deadliest poison known. When a handful of sweet flowers was given to her, her bosom scorched and shriveled the petals; when the rich perfume of her breath went among a swarm of insects, a score fell dead about her. A pet humming-bird entering her atmosphere, shuddered, hung for a moment in the air, then dropped in its final agony. Her love was poison; her embrace death. This tale has held a place in literature because it stands for men of evil all compact, whose presence has consumed integrities and exhaled iniquities. Happily the forces that bless are always more numerous and more potent than those that blight. Cast a bushel of chaff and one grain of wheat into the soil and nature will destroy all the chaff but cause the one grain of wheat to usher in rich harvests.

As a force-producer, man's primary influence is voluntary in nature. This is the capacity of purposely bringing all the soul's powers to bear upon society. It is the foundation of all instruction. The parent influences the child this way or that. The artist-master plies his pupil. The brave general or discoverer inspires and stimulates his men by multiform motives. The charioteer holds the reins, guides his steeds, restrains or lifts the scourge. Similarly man holds the reins of influence over man, and is himself in turn guided. So friend shapes and molds friend. This is what gives its meaning to conversation, oratory, journalism, reforms. Each man stands at the center of a great network of voluntary influence for good. Through words, bearing and gesture, he sends out his energies. Oftentimes a single speech has effected great reforms. Oft one man's act has deflected the stream of the centuries. Full oft a single word has been like a switch that turns a train from the route running toward the frozen North, to a track leading into the tropic South.

Not seldom has a youth been turned from the way of integrity by the influence of a single friend. Endowed as man is, the weight of his being effects the most astonishing results. Witness Stratton's conversation with the drunken bookbinder whom we know as John B. Gough, the apostle of temperance. Witness Moffat's words that changed David Livingstone, the weaver, into David Livingstone, the savior of Africa. Witness Garibaldi's words fashioning the Italian mob into the conquering army. Witness Garrison and Beecher and Phillips and John Bright. Rivers, winds, forces of fire and steam are impotent compared to those energies of mind and heart, that make men equal to transforming whole communities and even nations. Who can estimate the soul's conscious power? Who can measure the light and heat of last summer? Who can gather up the rays of the stars? Who can bring together the odors of last year's orchards? There are no mathematics for computing the influence of man's voluntary thought, affection and aspiration upon his fellows.

Man has also an unpurposed influence. Power goes forth without his distinct volition. Like all centers of energy, the soul does its best work automatically. The sun does not think of lifting the mist from the ocean, yet the vapor moves skyward. Often man is ignorant of what he accomplishes upon his fellows, but the results are the same. He is surcharged with energy. Accomplishing much by plan, he does more through unconscious weight of personality. In wonder-words we are told the apostle purposely wrought deeds of mercy upon the poor. Yet through his shadow falling on the weak and sick as he passed by, he unconsciously wrought health and hope in men. In like manner it is said that while Jesus Christ was seeking to comfort the comfortless, involuntarily virtue went out of him to strengthen one who did but touch the hem of his garment. Character works with or without consent. The selfish man fills his office with a malign atmosphere; his very presence chills like a cold, clammy day. Suspicious people fill all the circle in which they live with envy and jealousy. Moody men distribute gloom and depression; hopelessness drains off high spirits as cold iron draws the heat from the hand. Domineering men provoke rebellion and breed endless irritations.

Great hearts there are also among men; they carry a volume of manhood; their presence is sunshine, their coming changes our climate; they oil the bearings of life; their shadow always falls behind them; they make right living easy. Blessed are the happiness-makers!--they represent the best forces in civilization. They are to the heart and home what the honeysuckle is to the door over which it clings. These embodied gospels interpret Christianity. Jenny Lind explains a sheet of printed music--and a royal Christian heart explains, and is more than a creed. Little won-

unlighted candles; latent light is there; if they were only kindled and set burning they would be lights indeed.  What God asks for is luminous Christians and living gospels.

Another form of influence continues after death, and may be called unconscious immortality or conserved social energy.  Personality is organized into instruments, tools, books, institutions.  Over these forms of activity death and years have no power for destroying.  The swift steamboat and the flying train tell us that Watt and Stephenson are still toiling for men.  Every foreign cablegram reminds us that Cyrus Field has just returned home.  The merchant who organizes a great business sends down to the generations his personality, prudence, wisdom and executive skill.  The names of inventors may now be on moldering tombstones, but their busy fingers are still weaving warm textures for the world's poor.  The gardener of Hampton court, who, in old age, wished to do yet one more helpful deed, and planted with elms and oaks the roadway leading to the historic house, still lives in those columnar trees, and all the long summer through distributes comfort and refreshment.  Every man who opens up a roadway into the wilderness; every engineer throwing a bridge over icy rivers for weary travelers; every builder rearing abodes of peace, happiness and refinement for his generation; every smith forging honest plates that hold great ships in time of storm, every patriot that redeems his land with blood; every martyr forgotten and dying in his dungeon that freedom might never perish; every teacher and discoverer who has gone into lands of fever and miasma to carry liberty, intelligence and religion to the ignorant, still walks among men, working for society and is unconsciously immortal.

This is fame.  Life hath no holier ambition.  Some there are who, denied opportunity, have sought out those ambitious to learn, and, educating them, have sent their own personality out through artists, jurists or authors they have trained.  Herein is the test of the greatness of editor or statesman or merchant.  He has so incarnated his ideas or methods in his helpers that, while his body is one, his spirit has many-shaped forms; so that his journal, or institution, or party feels no jar nor shock in his death, but moves quietly forward because he is still here living and working in those into whom his spirit is incarnated.  Death ends the single life, but our multiplied life in others survives.

The supreme example of atmosphere and influence is Jesus Christ. His was a force mightier than intellect. Wherever he moved a light ne'er seen on land nor sea shone on man. It was more than eminent beauty or supreme genius. His scepter was not through cunning of brain or craft of hand; reality was his throne. "Therefore," said Charles Lamb, "if Shakespeare should enter the room we should rise and greet him uncovered, but kneeling meet the Nazarene." His gift cannot be bought nor commanded; but his secret and charm may be ours. Acceptance, obedience, companionship with him--these are the keys of power. The legend is, that so long as the Grecian hero touched the ground, he was strong; and measureless the influence of him who ever dwells in Christ's atmosphere. Man grows like those he loves. If great men come in groups, there is always a greater man in the midst of the company from whom they borrowed eminence--Socrates and his disciples; Cromwell and his friends; Coleridge and his company; Emerson and the Boston group; high over all the twelve disciples and the Name above every name. Perchance, in vision-hour, over against the man you are he will show you the man he would fain have you become; thereby comes greatness. For value is not in iron, but in the pattern that molds it; beauty is not in the pigments, but in the ideal that blends them; strength is not in the stone or marble, but in the plan of architect; greatness is not in wisdom, nor wealth, nor skill, but in the divine Christ who works up these raw materials of character. Forevermore the secret of eminence is the secret of the Messiah.

# LIFE'S GREAT HEARTS, AND THE HELPFULNESS OF THE HIGHER MANHOOD.

"Heaven doth with us as we with torches do,
Not light them for themselves, for if our virtues
Did not go forth of us, 'twere all alike
As if we had them not.  Spirits are not finely touched
But to fine issues, nor Nature never lends
The smallest scruple of her excellence,
But, like a thrifty goddess, she determines
Herself the glory of a creditor--
Both thanks and use."--*Measure for Measure*.

"A man was born, not for prosperity, but to suffer for the benefit of others, like the noble rock maple, which, all round our villages, bleeds for the service of man."--*Emerson*.

"Everything cries out to us that we must renounce.  Thou must go without, go without!  That is the everlasting song which every hour, all our life through, hoarsely sings to us:  Die, and come to life; for so long as this is not accomplished thou art but a troubled guest upon an earth of gloom."--*Goethe*.

The oases in the Arabian desert lie under the lee of long ridges of rock.  The high cliffs extending from north to south are barriers against the drifting sand.  Standing on the rocky summit the seer Isaiah beheld a sea whose yellow waves stretched to the very horizon. By day the winds were still, for the pitiless Asiatic sun made the desert a furnace whose air rose upward.  But when night falls the wind rises. Then the sand begins to drift. Soon every object lies buried under yellow flakes. Anon, sandstorms arise. Then the sole hope for man is to fall upon his face; the sky rains bullets. Then appears the ministry of the rocks. They stay the drifting sand. To the yellow sea they say: "Thus far, but no farther." Desolation is held back. Soon the land under the lee of the rocks becomes rich. It is fed by springs that seep out of the cliffs. It becomes a veritable oasis with figs and olives and vineyards and aromatic shrubs. Here dwell the sheik and his flocks. Hither come the caravans seeking refreshment. In all the Orient no spot so beautiful as the oasis under the shadow of the rocks. Long centuries ago, while Isaiah rejoiced under the beneficent ministry of these cliffs, his thoughts went out from dead rocks to living men. In his vision he saw good men as Great Hearts, to whom crowded close the weak and ignorant, seeking protection. Sheltered thereby barren lives were nourished into bounty and beauty. With leaping heart and streaming eyes he cried out; "O, what a desert is life but for the ministry of the higher manhood! To what shall I liken a good man? A man shall be as the shadow of a great rock in a weary land; a shelter in the time of storm!"

Optimists always, we believe God's world is a good world. Joy is more than sorrow; happiness outweighs misery; the reasons for living are more numerous than the reasons against it. But let the candid mind confess that life hath aspects very desert-like. Today prosperity grows like a fruitful tree; to-morrow adversity's hot winds wither every leaf. God plants companion, child, or friend in the life-garden; but death blasts the tree under which the soul finds shelter; then begins the desert pilgrimage. Soon comes loss of health; then the wealth of Croesus availeth not for refreshing sleep, and the wisdom of Solomon is vanity and vexation of spirit. The common people, too, know blight and blast; their life is full of mortal toil and strife, its fruitage grief and pain. Temptations and evil purposes are the chief blights. When the fiery passion hath passed the soul is like a city swept by a conflagration. Each night we go before the judgment seat. Reason hears the case; memory gives evidence; conscience convicts, each faculty goes to the left; self-respect pushes us out of paradise into the desert; and the angels of our better nature guard the gates with flaming swords.

A journey among men is like a journey through some land after the cyclone has made the village a heap and the harvest fields a waste. An outlook upon the generations reminds us of a highway along which the retreating army has passed, leaving abandoned guns and silent cannon with men dead and dying. Travelers from tropical Mexico describe ruined cities and lovely villages away from which civilized men journey, leaving temples and terraced gardens to moss and ivy. The deserted valleys are rich in tropic fruits and the climate soft and gentle. Yet Aztecs left the garden to journey northward into the deserts of Arizona and New Mexico. Often for the soul paradise is not before, but behind.

Shakespeare condenses all this in "King Lear." Avarice closes the palace doors against the white-haired King. Greed pushes him into the night to wander o'er the wasted moor, an exiled king, uncrowned and uncared for. In such hours garden becomes desert. This is the drama of man's life. The soul thirsts for sympathy. It hungers for love. Baffled and broken it seeks a great heart. For the pilgrim multitudes Moses was the shadow on a great rock in a weary land. For poor, hunted David, Jonathan was a covert in time of storm. Savonarola, Luther, Cromwell sheltered perishing multitudes. Solitary in the midst of the vale in which death will soon dig a grave for each of us stands the immortal Christ, "the shadow of a great rock in a weary land."

That Infinite Being who hath made man in his own image hath endowed the soul with full power to transform the desert into an oasis. The soul carries wondrous implements. It is given to reason to carry fertility where ignorance and fear and superstition have wrought desolation. It is given to inventive skill to search out wellsprings and smite rocks into living water. It is given to affection to hive sweetness like honeycombs. It is given to wit and imagination to produce perpetual joy and gladness. It is given to love in the person of a Duff, a Judson, and a Xavier to transform dark continents. Great is the power of love! "No abandoned boy in the city, no red man in the mountains, no negro in Africa can resist its sweet solicitude. It undermines like a wave, it rends like an earthquake, it melts like a fire, it inspires like music, it binds like a chain, it detains like a good story, it cheers like a sunbeam." No other power is immeasurable. For things have only partial influence over living men. Forests, fields, skies, tools, occupations, industries--these all stop in the outer court of the soul. It is given to affection alone to enter the sacred inner precincts. But once the good man comes his power is irresistible. Witness Arnold among the schoolboys at Rugby. Witness Garibaldi and his peasant soldiers. Witness the Scottish chief and his devoted clan. Witness artist pupils inflamed by their masters. What a noble group is that headed by Horace Mann, Garrison, Phillips and Lincoln! General Booth belongs to a like group. What a ministry of mercy and fertility and protection have these great hearts wrought! Great hearts become a shelter in time of storm.

All social reforms begin with some great heart. Much now is being said of the destitution in the poorer districts of great cities. Dante saw a second hell deeper than hell itself. Each great modern city hath its inferno. Here dwell costermongers, rag-pickers and street-cleaners; here the sweater hath his haunts. Huge rookeries and tenements, whose every brick exudes filth, teem with miserable folk. Each room has one or more families, from the second cellar at the bottom to the garret at the top. No greensward, no park, no blade of grass. Whole districts are as bare of beauty as an enlarged ash-heap. Here children are "spawned, not born, and die like flies." Here men and women grow bitter. Here anarchy grows rank. And to such a district in one great city has gone a man of the finest scholarship and the highest position, to become the friend of the poor. With him is his bosom friend, having wealth and culture, with pictures, marbles and curios. Every afternoon they invite several hundred poor women to spend an hour in the conservatory among the flowers. Every evening with stereopticon they take a thousand boys or men upon a journey to Italy or Egypt or Japan. The kindergartens, public schools and art exhibits cause these women and children to forget for a time their misery. One hour daily is redeemed from sorrow to joy by beautiful things and kindly surroundings. Love and sympathy have sheltered them from life's fierce heat. Bitter lives are slowly being sweetened. Springs are being opened in the desert. These great hearts have become "the shadow of a great rock in a weary land."

The Russian reformer, novelist and philanthropist, had an experience that profoundly influenced his career. Famine had wrought great suffering in Russia. One day the good poet passed a beggar on the street corner. Stretching out gaunt hands, with blue lips and watery eyes, the miserable creature asked an alms. Quickly the author felt for a copper. He turned his pockets inside out. He was without purse or ring or any gift. Then the kind man took the beggar's hand in both of his and said: "Do not be angry with me, brother, I have nothing with me!" The gaunt face lighted up; the man lifted his bloodshot eyes; his blue lips parted in a smile. "But you called me brother--that was a great gift." Returning an hour later he found the smile he had kindled still lingered on the beggar's face. His body had been cold; kindness had made his heart warm. The good man was as a covert in time of storm. History and experience exhibit now and then a man as unyielding as rock in friendships. Years ago a gifted youth began his literary career. Wealth, travel, friends, all good gifts were his. One day a friend handed him a telegram containing news of his father's death. Then the mother faded away. The youth was alone in the world. In that hour evil companions gathered around him. They spoiled him of his fresh innocency. They taught the delicate boy to listen to salacity without blushing. Soon coarse quips and rude jests ceased to shock him. He thought to "see life" by seeing the wrecks of manhood and womanhood. But does one study architecture by visiting hovels and squalid cabins? Is not studying architecture seeing the finest mansions and galleries and cathedrals? So to see life is to see manhood at its best and womanhood when carried up to culture and beauty.

Wasting his fortune this youth wasted also his friendships. One man loved him for his father's sake. For several years every Saturday night witnessed this man of oak and rock going from den to den looking for his old friend's boy. One day he wrote the youth a letter telling him, whether or not he found him, so long as he lived he would be looking for him every Saturday night in hope of redeeming him again to integrity. What nothing else could do love did. Kindness wrought its miracle. Clasping hands the man and boy climbed back again to the heights. At first the integrity was at best a poor, sickly plant. But his friend was a refuge in time of storm. A good man became the shadow of a great rock in life's weary land.

Our age is specially interested in the relation of happiness to the street, the market and counting-room. We have not yet acknowledged the responsibility of strength. Not always have our giant minds confessed the debt of power to weakness; the debt of wisdom to ignorance; the debt of wealth to poverty; the debt of holiness to iniquity. Jesus Christ was the first to incarnate this principle. By so much as the parent is wiser than the babe for building a protecting shield for happiness and well-being, by that much is the mother indebted to her babe. Why is one man more successful than another in the street's fierce conflict? Because he has more resources; is prudent, thrifty, quick to seize upon opportunity, sagacious, keen of judgment. All these qualities are birth-gifts. The ancestral foothills slope upward toward the mountain-minded. And what do these distinguished mental qualities involve?

Recognizing the responsibility of men of leisure and wealth, John Ruskin said: "Shall one by breadth and sweep of sight gather some branch of the commerce of the country into one great cobweb of which he is himself to be the master spider, making every thread vibrate with the points of his claws, and commanding every avenue with the facets of his eyes?" Shall the industrial or political giant say: "Here is the power in my hand; weakness owes me a debt? Build a mound here for me to be throned upon. Come, weave tapestries for my feet that I may tread in silk and purple; dance before me that I may be glad, and sing sweetly to me that I may slumber. So shall I live in joy and die in honor." Rather than such an honorable death, it were better that the day perish wherein such strength was born. Rather let the great mind become also the great heart, and stretch out his scepter over the heads of the common people that stoop to its waving. "Let me help you subdue the obstacle that baffled our fathers, and put away the plagues that consume our children. Let us together water these dry places; plow these desert moons; carry this food to those who are in hunger; carry this light to those who are in darkness; carry this life to those who are in death."

Superiority is to make erring men unerring and slow minds swift. Then, indeed, comes the better day--pray God it be not far off--when strength uses its wealth as the net of the sacred fisher to gather souls of men out of the deep.

In overplus of strength we have the measure of a man's greatness. Soul-power is resource for finding and feeding the hidden springs of life and thought in others. Not all have the same capacity. The Lord of the vineyard still sends into the white fields ten-talent men, two-talent men and one-talent men. Each hath his own task, and each must grasp the handle of his own being. Genius is widely distributed. Not many Platos--only one, and then a thousand lesser minds look up to him and learn to think. Not many Dantes--one, and a thousand poets tune their lyres to his and catch its notes. Not many Raphaels--one, and a thousand aspiring artists look up to him and are lifted by the look. Not many royal hearts--great magazines of kindness. Few are great in heart-power, effulging all sweet and generous qualities. Happy the community blessed with, a few great hearts and a few great minds. One such will civilize a whole community.

Classic literature charmed our childhood with the story of an Arabian sheik. He dwelt in an oasis near the edge of the desert. Wealth was his, with flocks and herds and wedges of gold. One night sleep forsook his couch. Yet the gurgle of falling water was in his ear. The odors of the vineyard were in his nostril; and to-morrow his servants would begin to gather the abundant harvest. Ten miles away ran the track of the caravan where his herdsmen had found a traveler dead from the fierce heat of the desert. Yonder the desert and a dying traveler; here an oasis with living water. Then the sheik arose; he bade his servants fill two leathern water-bottles and bring a basket full of figs and grapes. The next day a caravan came to a booth protecting two water-bottles sunk in the sand. Beside them were bunches of fruit. On a roll were these words: "While God gives me life each day shall a man be--as springs of water in a desert place." This beautiful story interprets for us the ministry of the higher manhood, as the great heart becomes the shadow of a great rock in a weary land.

This law of human helpfulness asks each man to carry himself so as to bless and not blight men, to make and not mar them. Besides the great ends of attaining character here and immortality hereafter, we are bound to so administer our talents as to make right living easy and smooth for others. Happy is he whose soul automatically oils all the machinery of the home, the market and the street. And this ambition to be universally helpful must not be a transient and occasional one--here and there an hour's friendship, a passing hint of sympathy, a transient gleam of kindness. Heart helpfulness is to enter into the fundamental conceptions of our living. With vigilant care man is to expel every element that vexes or irritates or chafes just as the husbandman expels nettles and poison ivy from fruitful gardens.

For nothing is so easily wrecked as the soul. As mechanisms go up toward complexity, delicacy increases. The fragile vase is ruined by a single tap. A chance blow destroys the statue. A bit of sand ruins the delicate mechanism. But the soul is even more sensitive to injury. It is marred by a word or a look. Men are responsible for the ruin they work unthinkingly! To-day the engine drops a spark behind it. To-morrow that engine is a thousand miles away. Yet the spark left behind is now a column of fire mowing down the forests. And that devastating column belongs not to another, but to that engine that hath journeyed far. Thus the evil man does lives after him. The condemnation of life is that a man hath carried friction and stirred up malign elements and sowed fiery discords, so that the gods track him by the swath of destruction he hath cut through life. The praise of life is that a man hath exhaled bounty and stimulus and joy and gladness wherever he journeys. To-day noble examples and ten thousand precepts unite in urging every one to become a great heart. Every individual must bring together his little group of pilgrim friends, companions, employes, using whatever he has of wisdom and skill for guiding those who follow him on their desert march. For happiness is through helpfulness. Every morning let us build a booth to shelter someone from life's fierce heat. Every noon let us dig some life-spring for thirsty lips. Every night let us be food for the hungry and shelter for the cold and naked. The law of the higher manhood asks man to be a great heart, the shadow of a rock in a weary land.

# THE INVESTMENT OF TALENT AND ITS RETURN.

"The universal blunder of this world is in thinking that there are certain persons put into the world to govern and certain others to obey. Everybody is in this world to govern and everybody to obey. There are no benefactors and no beneficiaries in distinct classes. Every man is at once both benefactor and beneficiary. Every good deed you do you ought to thank your fellowman for giving you an opportunity to do; and they ought to be thankful to you for doing it."--*Phillips Brooks*.

"Pity is love and something more; love at its utmost."--*T. T. Munger, "Freedom of Faith."*

"The great idea that the Bible is the history of mankind's deliverance from all tyranny, outward as well as inward, of the Jews, as the one free constitutional people among a world of slaves and tyrants, of their ruin, as the righteous fruit of a voluntary return to despotism; of the New Testament, as the good news that freedom, brotherhood, equality, once confided only to Judea and to Greece, and dimly seen even there, was henceforth to be the right of all mankind, the law of all society--who was there to tell me that? Who is there now to go forth and tell it to the millions who have suffered and doubted and despaired like me, and turn the hearts of the disobedient to the wisdom of the just, before the great and terrible day of the Lord come? Again I ask--who will go forth and preach that gospel and save his native land?"--*Charles Kingsley, "Alton Locke."*

In all ages man has been stimulated to sowing by the certainty of reaping. Tomorrow's sheaves and shoutings support to-day's tearful sowing. Certainty of victory wins battles before they are fought. Armed with confidence patriots have beaten down stone castles with naked fists. Uncertainty makes the heart sick, takes nerve out of arm and tension out of thought. The mere rumor of war along the border-lines of nations destroys enterprise and industry. Men will not plow if war-horses are to trample down the ripe grain. Men will not build if the enemy are to warm hands over blazing rafters. Why should the husbandman plant vines if others are to wrest away his fruit? The individual and the race need the stimulus of hope and a rational basis of security that nothing shall cut the connection between the causes sown and the effects to be reaped. Therefore, the divine word: "Send forth thy gift and talent, and nature and providence shall invest it securely and give the talent back with interest and increase."

What a promise for civilization was that of Christ: "Give and it shall be given unto you!" Let the husbandman give his seed to the furrows; soon the furrows will give back big bundles into the sower's arms. Let the vintner give the sweat of his brow to the vines; soon the vines will give back the rich purple floods. Give thy thought, O husbandman! to the wild rice; soon nature will give back the rice plump wheat. Give thyself, O inventor! to the raw ores, and nature will give thee the forceful tools. Give thyself, O reformer! to the desert world; soon the world-desert will be given back a world-garden. Give sparingly to nature, and sparingly shalt thou receive again. Give bountifully, and bounty shall be given back. Give scant thought and drag but one plank to the stream, and thou shalt receive only a narrow bridge across the brook. Give abundant thought to wires and cables and buttresses, and nature will give the bridge across the Firth of Forth. Give God thy one talent and, investing it, he returns ten. Give the cup of cold water and thou shalt have rivers of water of life. Share thy crust and thy cloak, and thou shall have banquet and robe and house of many mansions. This is the pledge of nature and God: "Give, and good measure pressed down and shaken together, shalt thou receive of celestial reapers." The history of progress is the history of Christ's challenge and man's response.

Christianity deals in universal. Its principles are not local nor racial nor temporary. They are meridian lines taking in all forces, men and movements. Nature, too, saith: "Give and it shall be given unto you." The sun gives heat to the forests, and afterward the burning coal and tree give heat back to the heavens; the arctics give icebergs and frigid streams for cooling the fierce tropics, and the tropics give back the warm Gulf Stream. The soil in the spring gives its treasures to the growing tree, and in the autumn the tree gives its leaves to make the soil richer and deeper. Personal also is this principle. Give thy body food and thy body will give thee mental strength. Give thy blow to the ax, and the ax will return the fallen tree, with strong tools for thy arm. Give thy brain sleep and rest and thy brain will give thy thought nimbleness. Give thy mind to rocks, and the rock pages will give thee wealth of wisdom. Give thy thought to the fire and water, and they will give thee an engine stronger than tamed lions. Give thy scrutiny to the thunderbolt leaping from the east to the west, and the lightnings shall give themselves back to thee as noiseless and gentle and obedient as the sunlight. Give thy mind to books and libraries, and the literature and lore of the ages will give thee the wisdom of sage and seer. Let some hero give his love and self-sacrificing service to the poor in prisons, and society will give him in return, monuments and grateful memory. Give thy obedience to conscience, and God, whom conscience serves, will give Himself to thee.

Being a natural principle, this law is also spiritual. Standing by his mother's knee each child hears the story of the echo. The boy visiting in the mountains, when he called aloud found that he was mocked by a hidden stranger boy. The insult made him very angry. So he shouted back insults and epithets. But each of these bad words was returned to him from the rocks above. With bitter tears the child returned to his mother, who sent him back to give the hidden stranger kind words and affectionate greetings. Lo! the stranger now echoed back his kindliness. Thus society echoes back each temperament and each career. Evermore man receives what he first gives to nature and society and God.

History is rich in interpretation of this principle. In every age man has received from society what he has given to society. This continent lay waiting for ages for the seed of civilization. At length the sower went forth to sow. Landing in midwinter upon a bleak coast, the fathers gave themselves to cutting roads, draining swamps, subduing grasses, rearing villages, until all the land was sown with the good seed of liberty and Christian civilization. Afterward, when tyranny threatened liberty, these worthies in defending their institutions gave life itself. Dying, they bequeathed their treasures to after generations. At length an enemy, darkling, lifted weapons for destroying. Would these who had received institutions nourished with blood, give life-blood in return? The uprising of 1861 is the answer. Then the people rose as one man, the plow stood in the furrow, the hammer fell from the hand, workroom and college hall were alike deserted--a half-million men laid down their lives upon many a battle-field. Similarly, the honor given to Washington during these last few days tells us that the patriot who gives shall receive. From the day when the young Virginian entered the Indian forests with Braddock to the day when he lay dying at Mount Vernon the patriot gave his health, his wealth, his time, his life, a living sacrifice through eight and forty years. Now every year the people, rising up early and sitting up late, rehearse to their children the story of his life and work. Having given himself, honor shall he receive through all the ages.

To Abraham Lincoln also came the word: "Give and thou shall receive!" Sitting in the White House the President proclaimed equal rights to black and white. Then, with shouts of joy, three million slaves entered the temple of liberty. But they bore the emancipator upon their shoulders and enshrined him forever in the temple of fame, where he who gave bountifully shall receive bountiful honor through all the ages. There, too, in the far-off past stands an uplifted cross. Flinging wide his arms this crowned sufferer sought to lift the world back to his Father's side. In life he gave his testimony against hypocrisy, Phariseeism and cruelty. For years he gave himself to the publican, the sinner, the prodigal, the poor in mind or heart, and so came at length to his pitiless execution. But, having given himself in abandon of love, the world straightway gave itself in return. Every one of his twelve disciples determined to achieve a violent death for the Christ who gave himself for them. Paul was beheaded in Rome. John was tortured in Patmos. Andrew and James were crucified in Asia. The rest were mobbed, or stoned, or tortured to death. And as years sped on man kept giving. Multitudes went forth, burning for him in the tropics, freezing for him in the arctics; threading for him the forest paths, braving for him the swamps, that they might serve his little ones. He gave himself for the world, and the world, in a passion of love, will yet give itself back to him.

Recently the officials of the commonwealth of Massachusetts and the noblest citizens of Boston assembled for celebrating the one hundredth anniversary of the birth of George Peabody. For a like purpose the citizens of London came together in banquet hall. Now, the banker had long been dead. Nor did he leave children to keep his name before the public.  How shall we account for two continents giving him such praise and fame?  George Peabody received from his fellows, because he first gave to his fellows.  To his genius for accumulation he added the genius of distribution.  His large gifts to Harvard and Yale, to Salem and Peabody, made to science and art as well as to philanthropy and religion, secured perpetual remembrance.  When the public credit of the State of Maryland was endangered, he negotiated $8,000,000 in London and gave his entire commission of $200,000 back to the State.  He who gave $3,500,000 for founding schools and colleges in the South for black and white, could not but receive honor and praise.  Therefore the eulogies pronounced by the legislators in Annapolis.  As a banker in London he was disturbed by the sorrows of the poor, and for months gave himself to an investigation of the tenement-house system, developing the Peabody Tenements, to which he gave $2,500,000, and helped 20,000 people to remove from dens into buildings that were light and sweet and wholesome.  Therefore when he died in London the English nation that had received from him gave to him, and, for the first time in history, the gates of Westminster Abbey were thrown open for the funeral services of a foreigner.  Therefore, the Prime Minister of England selected the swiftest frigate in the English navy for carrying his body back to his native land.  His generosity radiated in every direction, not in trickling rivulets, but in copious streams.  Bountifully he gave to men; therefore, through innumerable orations, sermons, editorials and toasts, men vied with each other in giving praise and honor back to Peabody, the benefactor of the people.

Society, always sensitive to generosity, is equally sensitive to selfishness.  He who treats his fellows as so many clusters to be squeezed into his cup, who spoils the world for self aggrandizement, finds at last that he has burglarized his own soul.  Here is a man who says: "Come right, come wrong, I will get gain."  Loving ease, he lashes himself to unceasing toil by day and night.  Needing rest on Sunday, he denies himself respite and scourges his jaded body and brain into new activities.  Every thought is a thread to be woven into a golden net.  He lifts his life to strike as miners lift their picks.  He swings his body as harvesters their scythes.  He will make himself an augur for boring, a chisel for drilling, a muck-rake for scratching, if only he may get gain.  He will sweat and swelter and burn in the tropics until malaria has made his face as yellow as gold, if thereby he can fill his purse, and for a like end he will shiver and ache in the arctics. He will deny his ear music, he will deny his mind culture, he will deny his heart friendship that he may coin concerts and social delights into cash. At length the shortness of breath startles him; the stoppage of blood alarms him. Then he retires to receive--what? To receive from nature that which he has given to nature. Once he denied his ear melody, and now taste in return denies him pleasure. Once he denied his mind books, and now books refuse to give him comfort. Once he denied himself friendship, and now men refuse him their love. Having received nothing from him, the great world has no investment to return to him. Such a life, entering the harbor of old age, is like unto a bestormed ship with empty coal bins, whose crew fed the furnace, first with the cargo and then with the furniture, and reached the harbor, having made the ship a burned-cut shell. God buries the souls of many men long years before their bodies are carried to the graveyard.

This principle tells us why nature and society are so prodigal with treasures to some men and so niggardly to others. What a different thing a forest is to different men! He who gives the ax receives a mast. He who gives taste receives a picture. He who gives imagination receives a poem. He who gives faith hears the "goings of God in the tree-tops." The charcoal-burner fronts an oak for finding out how many cords of wood are in it, as the Goths of old fronted peerless temples for estimating how many huts they could quarry from the stately pile.[1] But an artist curses the woodsman for making the tree food for ax and saw. It has become to him as sacred as the cathedral within which he bares his head. It is a temple where birds praise God. It is a harp with endless music for the summer winds. It fills his eye with beauty and his ear with rustling melodies.

For the poet that selfsame oak is enshrined in a thousand noble associations. It sings for him like a hymn; it shines like a vision; it suggests ships, storms and ocean battles; the spear of Launcelot, the forests of Arden; old baronial halls mellow with lights falling on oaken floors; King Arthur's banqueting chamber. To the scientist's thought the oak is a vital mechanism. By day and by night, the long summer through, it lifts tons of moisture and forces it into the wide-spreading branches, but without the rattle of huge engines. With what uproar and clang of iron hammers would stones be crushed that are dissolved noiselessly by the rootlets and recom-

---

1   Mod. Ptrs., Vol. 5, Chap. 1. The Earth--Veil Star papers: A Walk Among Trees.

posed in stems and boughs! What a vast laboratory is here, every root and leaf an expert chemist!

For other multitudes the earth has become only a huge stable; its fruit fodder; its granaries ricks, out of which men-cattle feed. These estimate a man's value according as he has lifted his ax upon tall trees and ravaged all the loveliness of creation; whose curse is the Nebuchadnezzar curse, giving to nature the tongue and hand, and receiving from nature grass; who are doomed to love the corn they grind, to hear only the roar of the whirlwind and the crash of the hail, never "the still small voice;" who see what is written in lamp-black and lightning; who think the clouds are for rain, and know not that they are chariots, thrones and celestial highways; that the sunset means something else than sleep, and the morning suggests something other than work. All these give nature only thought for food, and food only shall they receive from nature, until all their deeds are plowed down in dust. Give forth thy gift, young men and maidens, and according as thou givest thou shalt receive fruit, or picture, or poem, or temple, or ladder let down from heaven, or angel aspirations going up.

Conscience also receives its gifts and makes a return. Give thy body obedience and it will return happiness and health. Give overdrafts and excesses and it will return sleepless nights and suffering days. Man's sins are seeds, his sufferings harvests. Every action is embryonic, and according as it is right or wrong will ripen into sweet fruits of pleasure or poison fruits of pain. Some seeds hold two germs; and vice and penalty are wrapped up under one covering. Sins are self-registering and penalties are automatic. The brain keeps a double set of books, and at last visits its punishments. Conscience does not wait for society to ferret out iniquity, but daily executes judgment. Policemen may slumber and the judge may nod, but the nerves are always active, memory never sleeps, conscience is never off duty. The recoil of the gun bruises black the shoulder of him who holds it, and sin is a weapon that kills at both ends.

In the olden days, when the poisoner was in every palace, the Doge of Venice offered a reward for a crystal goblet that would break the moment a poison touched it. Perhaps the idea was suggested to the Prince because his soul already fulfilled the thought, for one drop of sin always shatters the cup of joy and wastes life's precious wine. How do events interpret this principle! One day Louis, King of France, was riding in the forest near his gorgeous and guilty palace of Versailles.  He met a peasant carrying a coffin.  "What did the man die of?" asked the King.  "Of hunger," answered the peasant.  But the sound of the hunt was in the King's ear, and he forgot the cry of want.  Soon the day came when the King stood before the guillotine, and with mute appeals for mercy fronted a mob silent as statues, unyielding as stone, grimly waiting to dip the ends of their pikes in regal blood.  He gave cold looks; he received cold steel.

Marie Antoinette, riding to Notre Dame for her bridal, bade her soldiers command all beggars, cripples and ragged people to leave the line of the procession.  The Queen could not endure for a brief moment the sight of those miserable ones doomed to unceasing squalor and poverty.  What she gave others she received herself, for soon, bound in an executioner's cart, she was riding toward the place of execution midst crowds who gazed upon her with hearts as cold as ice and hard as granite.  When Foulon was asked how the starving populace was to live he answered: "Let them eat grass."  Afterward, Carlyle says, the mob, maddened with rage, "caught him in the streets of Paris, hanged him, stuck his head upon a pike, filled his mouth with grass, amid shouts as of Tophet from a grass-eating people."  What kings and princes gave they received.  This is the voice of nature and conscience: "Behold, sin crouches at the door!"

This divine principle also explains man's attitude toward his fellows. The proverb says man makes his own world.  Each sees what is in himself, not what is outside.  The jaundiced eye yellows all it beholds.  The chameleon takes its color from the bark on which it clings.  Man gives his color to what his thought is fastened upon.  The pessimist's darkness makes all things dingy.  The youth disappointed with his European trip said he was a fool for going.  He was, for the reason that he was a fool before he started.  He saw nothing without, because he had no vision within.  He gave no sight, he received no vision.  An artist sees in each Madonna that which compels a rude mob to uncover in prayer, but the savage perceives only a colored canvas. Recently a foreign traveler, writing of his impressions of our city, described it to his fellows as a veritable hades.  But his fellow countryman, in a similar volume, recorded his impressions of our art, architecture and interest in education.  Each saw that for which he looked.

This principle explains man's attitude toward his God.  God governs rocks by force, animals by fear, savage man by force and fear, true men by hope and love. Man can take God at whatsoever level he pleases. He who by beastliness turns his body into a log will be held by gravity in one spot like a log. He who lives on a level with the animals will receive fear and law and lightnings. He who approaches God through laws of light and heat and electricity will find the world-throne occupied by an infinite Agassiz. Some approach God through physical senses. They behold his storms sinking ships, his tornadoes mowing down forests. These find him a huge Hercules; yet the Judge who seems cruel to the wicked criminal may seem the embodiment of gentleness and kindness to his obedient children. Man determines what God shall be to him. Each paints his own picture of Deity. Macbeth sees him with forked lightnings without and volcanic fires within. The pure in heart see him as the face of all-clasping Love. Give him thy heart and he will give thee love, effulgent love, like the affection of mother or lover or friend, only dearer than either. Give him thy ways, and he will overarch life's path as the heavens overarch the flowers, filling them with heat by day and yielding cooling dews by night. Give him but a flickering aspiration and he will give thee balm for the bruised reed and flame for the smoking flax. Give him the publican's prayer and he will give thee mercy like the wideness of the sea. Give his little ones but a cup of cold water and he will give thee to drink of the water of the river of life and bring thee to the banquet hall in the house of many mansions.

# VICARIOUS LIVES AS INSTRUMENTS OF SOCIAL PROGRESS.

Only he that uses shall even so much as keep. Unemployed strength steadily diminishes. The sluggard's arm grows soft and flabby. So, even in this lowest sphere, the law is inexorable. Having is using. Not using is losing. Idleness is paralysis. New triumphs must only dictate new struggles. If it be Alexander of Macedon, the Orontes must suggest the Euphrates, and the Euphrates the Indus. Always it must be on and on. One night of rioting in Babylon may arrest the conquering march. Genius is essentially athletic, resolute, aggressive, persistent. Possession is grip, that tightens more and more. Ceasing to gain, we begin to lose. Ceasing to advance, we begin to retrograde. Brief was the interval between Roman conquest of Barbarians, and Barbarian conquest of Rome. Blessed is the man who keeps out of the hospital and holds his place in the ranks. Blessed the man, the last twang of whose bow-string is as sharp as any that went before, sending its arrow as surely to the mark."-- *Roswell W. Hitchcock*.

The eleventh chapter of Hebrews has been called the picture-gallery of heroes. These patriots and martyrs who won our first battles for liberty and religion made nobleness epidemic. Oft stoned and mobbed in the cities they founded and loved, they fled into exile, where they wandered in deserts and mountains and caves and slept in the holes of the earth. Falling at last in the wilderness, it may be said that no man knoweth their sepulcher and none their names. But joyfully let us confess that the institutions most eminent and excellent in our day represent the very principles for which these martyrs died and, dying, conquered. For those heroes were the first to dare earth's despots. They won the first victory over every form of vice and sin. They wove the first threads of the flag of liberty and made it indeed the banner of the morning, for they dyed it crimson in their heart's-blood. In all the history of freedom there is no chapter comparable for a moment to the glorious achievements of these men of oak and rock. Their deeds shine on the pages of history like stars blazing in the night and their achievements have long been celebrated in song and story. "The angels of martyrdom and victory," says Mazzini, "are brothers; both extend protecting wings over the cradle of the future life."

Sometimes it has happened that the brave deed of a single patriot has rallied wavering hosts, flashed the lightning through the centuries, and kindled whole nations into a holy enthusiasm. The opposing legions of soldiers and inquisitors went down before the heroism of the early church as darkness flees before the advancing sunshine. Society admires the scholar, but man loves the hero. Wisdom shines, but bravery inspires and lifts. Though centuries have passed, these noble deeds still nourish man's bravery and endurance. It was not given to these leaders to enter into the fruits of their labors. Vicariously they died. With a few exceptions, their very names remain unknown. But let us hasten to confess that their vicarious suffering stayed the onset of despotism and achieved our liberty. They ransomed us from serfdom and bought our liberty with a great price. Compared to those, our bravest deeds do seem but brambles to the oaks at whose feet they grow.

Having made much of the principles of the solidarity of society, science is now engaged in emphasizing the principle of vicarious service and suffering. The consecrated blood of yesterday is seen to be the social and spiritual capital of to-day. Indeed, the civil, intellectual and religious freedom and hope of our age are only the moral courage and suffering of past ages, reappearing under new and resplendent forms. The social vines that shelter us, the civic bough whose clusters feed us, all spring out of ancient graves. The red currents of sacrifice and the tides of the heart have nourished these social growths and made their blossoms crimson and brilliant. Nor could these treasures have been gained otherwise. Nature grants no free favors. Every wise law, institution and custom must be paid for with corresponding treasure. Thought itself takes toll from the brain. To be loved is good, indeed; but love must be paid for with toil, endurance, sacrifice--fuel that feeds love's flame.

Generous giving to-day is a great joy; but it is made possible only by years of thrift and economy. The wine costs the clusters. The linen costs the flax. The furniture costs the forests. The heat in the house costs the coal in the cellar. Wealth costs much toil and sweat by day. Wisdom costs much study and long vigils by night. Leadership costs instant and untiring pains and service. Character costs the long, fierce conflict with vice and sin. When Keats, walking in the rose garden, saw the ground under the bushes all covered with pink petals, he exclaimed; "Next year the roses should be very red!" When Aeneas tore the bough from the myrtle tree, Virgil says the tree exuded blood. But this is only a poet's way of saying that civilization is a tree that is nourished, not by rain and snow, but by the tears and blood of the patriots and prophets of yesterday.

Fortunately, in manifold ways, nature and life witness to the universality of vicarious service and suffering. Indeed, the very basis of the doctrine of evolution is the fact that the life of the higher rests upon the death of the lower. The astronomers tell us that the sun ripens our harvests by burning itself up. Each golden sheaf, each orange bough, each bunch of figs, costs the sun thousands of tons of carbon. Geike, the geologist, shows us that the valleys grow rich and deep with soil through the mountains, growing bare and being denuded of their treasure. Beholding the valleys of France and the plains of Italy all gilded with corn and fragrant with deep grass, where the violets and buttercups wave and toss in the summer wind, travelers often forget that the beauty of the plains was bought, at a great price, by the bareness of the mountains. For these mountains are in reality vast compost heaps, nature's stores of powerful stimulants. Daily the heat swells the flakes of granite; daily the frost splits them; daily the rains dissolve the crushed stone into an impalpable dust; daily the floods sweep the rich mineral foods down into the starving valleys. Thus the glory of the mountains is not alone their majesty of endurance, but also their patient, passionate beneficence as they pour forth all their treasures to feed richness to the pastures, to wreathe with beauty each distant vale and glen, to nourish all waving harvest fields. This death of the mineral is the life of the vegetable.

If now we descend from the mountains to explore the secrets of the sea, Maury and Guyot show us the isles where palm trees wave and man builds his homes and cities midst rich tropic fruits. There scientists find that the coral islands were reared above the waves by myriads of living creatures that died vicariously that man might live. And everywhere nature exhibits the same sacrificial principle.

Our treasures of coal mean that vast forests have risen and fallen again for our factories and furnaces. Nobody is richer until somebody is poorer. Evermore the vicarious exchange is going on. The rock decays and feeds the moss and lichen. The moss decays to feed the shrub. The shrub perishes that the tree may have food and growth. The leaves of the tree fall that its boughs may blossom and bear fruit. The seeds ripen to serve the birds singing in all the boughs. The fruit falls to be food for man. The harvests lend man strength for his commerce, his government, his culture and conscience. The lower dies vicariously that the higher may live. Thus nature achieves her gifts only through vast expenditures.

It is said that each of the new guns for the navy costs $100,000. But the gun survives only a hundred explosions, so that every shot costs $1,000. Tyndall tells us that each drop of water sheathes electric power sufficient to charge 100,000 Leyden jars and blow the Houses of Parliament to atoms. Farraday amazes us by his statement of the energy required to embroider a violet or produce a strawberry. To untwist the sunbeam and extract the rich strawberry red, to refine the sugar, and mix its flavor, represents heat sufficient to run an engine from Liverpool to London or from Chicago to Detroit. But because nature does her work noiselessly we must not forget that each of her gifts also involves tremendous expenditure.

This law of vicarious service holds equally in the intellectual world. The author buys his poem or song with his life-blood. While traveling north from London midst a heavy snow-storm, Lord Bacon descended from his coach to stuff a fowl with snow to determine whether or not ice would preserve flesh. With his life the philosopher purchased for us the principle that does so much to preserve our fruits and foods through the summer's heat and lend us happiness and comfort. And Pascal, whose thoughts are the seeds that have sown many a mental life with harvests, bought his splendid ideas by burning up his brain. The professors who guided and loved him knew that the boy would soon be gone, just as those who light a candle in the evening know that the light, burning fast, will soon flicker out in the deep socket. One of our scientists foretells the time when, by the higher mathematics, it will be possible to compute how many brain cells must be torn down to earn a given sum of money; how much vital force each Sir William Jones must give in exchange for one of his forty languages and dialects; what percentage of the original vital force will be consumed in experiencing each new pleasure, or surmounting each new pain; how much nerve treasure it takes to conquer each temptation or endure each self-sacrifice. Too often society forgets that the song, law or reform has cost the health and life of the giver. Tradition says that, through much study, the Iliad cost Homer his eyes. There is strange meaning in the fact that Dante's face was plowed deep with study and suffering and written all over with the literature of sorrow.

To gain his vision of the hills of Paradise, Milton lost his vision of earth's beauteous sights and scenes. In explanation of the early death of Raphael and Burns, Keats and Shelley, it has been said that few great men who are poor have lived to see forty. They bought their greatness with life itself. A few short years ago there lived in a western state a boy who came up to his young manhood with a great, deep passion for the plants and shrubs. While other boys loved the din and bustle of the city, or lingered long in the library, or turned eager feet toward the forum, this youth plunged into the fields and forests, and with a lover's passion for his noble mistress gave himself to roots and seeds and flowers. While he was still a child he would tell on what day in March the first violet bloomed; when the first snowdrop came, and, going back through his years, could tell the very day in spring when the first robin sang near his window. Soon the boy's collection of plants appealed to the wonder of scholars. A little later students from foreign countries began to send him strange flowers from Japan and seeds from India. One midnight while he was lingering o'er his books, suddenly the white page before him was as red with his lifeblood as the rose that lay beside his hand. And when, after two years in Colorado, friends bore his body up the side of the mountains he so dearly loved, no scholar in all our land left so full a collection and exposition of the flowers of that distant state as did this dying boy. His study and wisdom made all to be his debtors. But he bought his wisdom with thirty years of health and happiness. We are rich only because the young scholar, with his glorious future, for our sakes made himself poor.

Our social treasure also is the result of vicarious service and suffering. Sailing along the New England coasts, one man's craft strikes a rock and goes to the bottom. But where his boat sank there the state lifts a danger signal, and henceforth, avoiding that rock, whole fleets are saved. One traveler makes his way through the forest and is lost. Afterward other pilgrims avoid that way. Experimenting with the strange root or acid or chemical, the scholar is poisoned and dies. Taught by his agonies, others learn to avoid that danger.

Only a few centuries ago the liberty of thought was unknown. All lips were padlocked. The public criticism of a baron meant the confiscation of the peasant's land; the criticism of the pope meant the dungeon; the criticism of the king meant death. Now all are free to think for themselves, to sift all knowledge and public teachings, to cast away the chaff and to save the precious wheat. But to buy this freedom blood has flowed like rivers and tears have been too cheap to count.

To achieve these two principles, called liberty of thought and liberty of speech, some four thousand battles have been fought. In exchange, therefore, for one of these principles of freedom and happiness, society has paid--not cash down, but blood down; vital treasure for staining two thousand battle-fields. To-day the serf has entered into citizenship and the slave into freedom, but the pathway along which the slave and serf have moved has been over chasms filled with the bodies of patriots and hills that have been leveled by heroes' hands. Why are the travelers through the forests dry and warm midst falling rains? Why are sailors upon all seas comfortable under their rubber coats? Warm are they and dry midst all storms, because for twenty years Goodyear, the discoverer of India rubber, was cold and wet and hungry, and at last, broken-hearted, died midst poverty.

Why is Italy cleansed of the plagues that devastated her cities a hundred years ago? Because John Howard sailed on an infected ship from Constantinople to Venice, that he might be put into a lazaretto and find out the clew to that awful mystery of the plague and stay its power. How has it come that the merchants of our western ports send ships laden with implements for the fields and conveniences for the house into the South Sea Islands? Because such men as Patteson, the pure-hearted, gallant boy of Eton College, gave up every prospect in England to labor amid the Pacific savages and twice plunged into the waters of the coral reefs, amid sharks and devil-fish and stinging jellies, to escape the flight of poisoned arrows of which the slightest graze meant horrible death, and in that high service died by the clubs of the very savages whom he had often risked his life to save--the memory of whose life did so smite the consciences of his murderers that they laid "the young martyr in an open boat, to float away over the bright blue waves, with his hands crossed, as if in prayer, and a palm branch on his breast." And there, in the white light, he lies now, immortal forever.

And why did the representatives of five great nations come together to destroy the slave trade in Africa, and from every coast come the columns of light to journey toward the heart of the dark continent and rim all Africa around with little towns and villages that glow like lighthouses for civilization?  Because one day Westminster Abbey was crowded with the great men of England, in the midst of whom stood two black men who had brought Livingstone's body from the jungles of Africa.  There, in the great Abbey, faithful Susi told of the hero who, worn thin as parchment through thirty attacks of the African fever, refused Stanley's overtures, turned back toward Ulala, made his ninth attempt to discover the head-waters of the Nile and search out the secret lairs of the slave-dealers, only to die in the forest, with no white man near, no hand of sister or son to cool his fevered brow or close his glazing eyes.  Faithful to the last to that which had been the great work of his life, he wrote these words with dying hand: "All I can add in my solitude is, may heaven's rich blessings come down on every one who would help to heal this open sore of the world!"  Why was it that in the ten years after Livingstone's death, Africa made greater advancement than in the previous ten centuries?  All the world knows that it was through the vicarious suffering of one of Scotland's noblest heroes.  And why is it that Curtis says that there are three American orations that will live in history--Patrick Henry's at Williamsburg, Abraham Lincoln's at Gettysburg and Wendell Philips' at Faneuil Hall?  A thousand martyrs to liberty lent eloquence to Henry's lips; the hills of Gettysburg, all billowy with our noble dead, exhaled the memories that anointed Lincoln's lips; while Lovejoy's spirit, newly martyred at Alton, poured over Wendell Phillips' nature the full tides of speech divine.  Vicarious suffering explains each of these immortal scenes.

Long, too, the scroll of humble heroes whose vicarious services have exalted our common life.  Recognizing this principle, Cicero built a monument to his slave, a Greek, who daily read aloud to his master, took notes of his conversation, wrote out his speeches and so lent the orator increased influence and power.  Scott also makes one of his characters bestow a gift upon an aged servant.  For, said the warrior, no master can ever fully recompense the nurse who cares for his children, or the maid who supplies their wants.  To-day each giant of the industrial realm is compassed about with a small army of men who stand waiting to carry out his slightest behests, relieve him of details, halve his burdens, while at the same time doubling his joys and rewards. Lifted up in the sight of the entire community the great man stands on a lofty pedestal builded out of helpers and aids. And though here and now the honors and successes all go to the one giant, and his assistants are seemingly obscure and unrecognized, hereafter and there honors will be evenly distributed, and then how will the great man's position shrink and shrivel!

Here also are the parents who loved books and hungered for beauty, yet in youth were denied education and went all their life through concealing a secret hunger and ambition, but who determined that their children should never want for education. That the boy, therefore, might go to college, these parents rose up early to vex the soil and sat up late to wear their fingers thin, denying the eye beauty, denying the taste and imagination their food, denying the appetite its pleasures. And while they suffer and wane the boy in college grows wise and strong and waxing great, comes home to find the parents overwrought with service and ready to fall on death, having offered a vicarious sacrifice of love.

And here are our own ancestors. Soon our children now lying in the cradles of our state will without any forethought of theirs fall heir to this rich land with all its treasures material--houses and vineyards, factories and cities; with all its treasures mental--library and gallery, school and church, institutions and customs. But with what vicarious suffering were these treasures purchased! For us our fathers subdued the continents and the kingdoms, wrought freedom, stopped the mouths of wolves, escaped the sword of savages, turned to flight armies of enemies, subdued the forests, drained the swamps, planted vineyards, civilized savages, reared schoolhouses, builded churches, founded colleges. For four generations they dwelt in cabins, wore sheepskins and goatskins, wandered about exploring rivers and forests and mines, being destitute, afflicted, tormented, because of their love of liberty, and for the slave's sake were slain with the sword--of whom this generation is not worthy. "And these all died not having received the promise," God having reserved that for us to whom it has been given to fall heir to the splendid achievements of our Christian ancestors.

And what shall we more say, save only to mention those whose early death as well as life was vicarious? What an enigma seems the career of those cut off while yet they stand upon life's threshold! How proud they made our hearts, standing forth all clothed with beauty, health and splendid promise! What a waste of power, what a robbery of love, seemed their early death! But slowly it has dawned upon us that the footsteps that have vanished walk with us more frequently than do our nearest friends. And the sound of the voice that is still instructs us in our dreams as no living voice ever can. The invisible children and friends are the real children. Their memory is a golden cord binding us to God's throne, and drawing us upward into the kingdom of light. Absent, they enrich us as those present cannot. And so the child who smiled upon us and then went away, the son and the daughter whose talents blossomed here to bear fruit above, the sweet mother's face, the father's gentle spirit--their going it was that set open the door of heaven and made on earth a new world. These all lived vicariously for us, and vicariously they died!

No deeply reflective nature, therefore, will be surprised that the vicarious principle is manifest in the Savior of the soul. Rejecting all commercial theories, all judicial exchanges, all imputations of characters, let us recognize the universality of this principle. God is not at warfare with himself. If he uses the vicarious principle in the realm of matter he will use it in the realm of mind and heart. It is given unto parents to bear not only the weakness of the child, but also his ignorance, his sins-- perhaps, at last, his very crimes. But nature counts it unsafe to permit any wrong to go unpunished. Nature finds it dangerous to allow the youth to sin against brain or nerve or digestion without visiting sharp penalties upon the offender. Fire burns, acids eat, rocks crush, steam scalds--always, always. Governments also find it unsafe to blot out all distinctions between the honest citizen and the vicious criminal. The taking no notice of sin keeps iniquity in good spirits, belittles the sanctity of law and blurs the conscience.

With God also penalties are warnings. His punishments are thorn hedges, safe- guarding man from the thorns and thickets where serpents brood, and forcing his feet back into the ways of wisdom and peace. For man's integrity and happiness, therefore, conscience smites and is smiting unceasingly. Therefore, Eugene Aram dared not trust himself out under the stars at night, for these stars were eyes that blazed and blazed and would not relent. But why did not the murderer, Eugene Aram, forgive himself? When Lady Macbeth found that the water in the basin would not wash off the red spots, but would "the multitudinous seas incarnadine," why did not Macbeth and his wife forgive each other? Strange, passing strange, that Shakespeare thought volcanic fires within and forked lightning without were but the symbols of the storm that breaks upon the eternal orb of each man's soul. If David cannot forgive himself, if Peter cannot forgive Judas, who can forgive sins? "Perhaps the gods may," said Plato to Socrates. "I do not know," answered the philosopher. "I do not know that it would be safe for the gods to pardon." So the poet sends Macbeth out into the black night and the blinding storm to be thrown to the ground by forces that twist off trees and hiss among the wounded boughs and bleeding branches.

For poor Jean Valjean, weeping bitterly for his sins, while he watched the boy play with the buttercups and prayed that God would give him, the red and horny-handed criminal, to feel again as he felt when he pressed his dewy cheek against his mother's knee--for Jean Valjean is there no suffering friend, no forgiving heart? Is there no bosom where poor Magdalene can sob out her bitter confession? What if God were the soul's father! What if he too serves and suffers vicariously! What if his throne is not marble but mercy! What if nature and life do but interpret in the small this divine principle existing in the large in him who is infinite![2] What if Calvary is God's eternal heartache, manifest in time! What if, sore-footed and heavy-hearted, bruised with many a fall, we should come back to the old home, from which once we fled away, gay and foolish prodigals! The time was when, as small boys and girls, with blinding tears, we groped toward the mother's bosom and sobbed out our bitter pain and sorrow with the full story of our sin. What if the form on Calvary were like the king of eternity, toiling up the hill of time, his feet bare, his locks all wet with the dew of night, while he cries: "Oh, Absalom! my son, my son, Absalom!" What if we are Absalom, and have hurt God's heart! Reason staggers. Groping, trusting, hoping, we fall blindly on the stairs that slope through darkness up to God. But, falling, we fall into the arms of Him who hath suffered vicariously for man from the foundation of the world.

---

2   *Eternal Atonement*, p. 11.

# GENIUS, AND THE DEBT OF STRENGTH.

Paul says: 'I am a debtor.' But what had he received from the Greeks that he was bound to pay back? Was he a disciple of their philosophy? He was not. Had he received from their bounty in the matter of art? No. One of the most striking things in history is the fact that Paul abode in Athens and wrote about it, without having any impression made upon his imaginative mind, apparently, by its statues, its pictures or its temples. The most gorgeous period of Grecian art poured its light on his path, and he never mentioned it. The New Testament is as dead to art-beauty as though it had been written by a hermit in an Egyptian pyramid who had never seen the light of sun. Then what did he owe the Greeks? Not philosophy, not art, and certainly not religion, which was fetichism. Not a debt of literature, nor of art, nor of civil polity; not a debt of pecuniary obligation; not an ordinary debt. He had nothing from all these outside sources. The whole barbaric world was without the true knowledge of God. He had that knowledge and he owed it to every man who had it not. All the civilized world was, in these respects, without the true inspiration; and he owed it to them simply because they did not have it; and his debt to them was founded on this law of benevolence of which I have been speaking, which is to supersede selfishness, and according to which those who have are indebted to those who have not the world over."--*Henry Ward Beecher*.

Booksellers rank "Quo Vadis" as one of the most popular books of the day. In that early era persecution was rife and cruelty relentless. It was the time of Caligula, who mourned that the Roman people had not one neck, so that he could cut it off at a single blow; of Nero, whose evening garden parties were lighted by the forms of blazing Christians; of Vespasian, who sewed good men in skins of wild beasts to be worried to death by dogs. In that day faith and death walked together.

Fulfilling such dangers, the disciples came together secretly at midnight. But the spy was abroad, and despite all precautions, from time to time brutal soldiers discovered the place of meeting, and, bursting in, dragged the worshipers off to prison. Then a cruel stratagem was adopted that looked to the discovery of those who secretly cherished faith. A decree went forth forbidding the jailer to furnish food, making the prisoners 'dependent' upon friends without.

To come forward as a friend of these endungeoned was to incur the risk of arrest and death, while to remain in hiding was to leave friends to die of starvation. Then men counted life not dear unto themselves. Heroism became a contagion. Even children dared death. An old painting shows the guard awakened at midnight and gazing with wonder upon a little child thrusting food between the iron bars to its father. In the darkness the soldiers sleeping in the corridors heard the rustling garments of some maiden or mother who loved life itself less than husband or friend. These tides of sympathy made men strong against torture; old men lifted joyful eyes toward those above them. Loving and beloved, the disciples shared their burdens, and those in the prison and those out of it together went to fruitful martyrdom.

When the flames of persecution had swept by and, for a time, good men had respite, Apollos recalled with joy the heroism of those without the prison who remembered the bonds of those within. With leaping heart he called before his mind the vast multitudes in all ages who so fettered through life--men bound by poverty and hedged in by ignorance; men baffled and beaten in life's fierce battle, bearing burdens of want and wretchedness, and by the heroism of the past he urged all men everywhere to fulfill that law of sympathy that makes hard tasks easy and heavy burdens light. Let the broad shoulders stoop to lift the load with weakness; let the wise and refined share the sorrows of the ignorant; let those whose health and gifts make them the children of freedom be abroad daily on missions of mercy to those whose feet are fettered; so shall life be redeemed out of its woe and want and sin through the Christian sympathy of those who "remember men in the bonds as bound with them."

Rejoicing in all of life's good things, let us confess that in our world-school the divine teachers are not alone happiness and prosperity, but also uncertainty and suffering, defeat and death. Inventors with steel plates may make warships proof against bombs, but no man hath invented an armor against troubles. The arrows of calamity are numberless, falling from above and also shot up from beneath. Like Achilles, each man hath one vulnerable spot. No palace door is proof against phantoms. Each prince's palace and peasant's cottage holds at least one bond-slave. Byron, with his club-foot, counted himself a prisoner pacing between the walls of his narrow dungeon. Keats, struggling against his consumption, thought his career that of the galley-slave. The mother, fastened for years to the couch of her crippled child, is bound by cords invisible, indeed, but none the less powerful. Nor is the bondage always physical. Here is the man who made his way out of poverty and loneliness toward wealth and position, yet maintained his integrity through all the fight, and stood in life's evening time possessed of wealth, but in a moment saw it crash into nothing and fell under bondage to poverty. And, here is some Henry Grady, a prince among men, the leader of the new South, his thoughts like roots drinking in the riches of the North; his speech like branches dropping bounty over all the tropic states, seeming to be the one indispensable man of his section, but who in the midst of his career is smitten and, dying, left his pilgrim band in bondage.

Here is Sir William Napier writing, "I am now old and feeble and miserable; my eyes are dim, very dim, with weeping for my lost child," and went on bound midst the thick shadows. Or here are the man and woman, set each to each like perfect music unto noble words, and one is taken--but Robert Browning was left to dwell in such sorrow that for a time he could not see his pen for the thick darkness. Here is the youth who by one sin fell out of man's regard, and struggling upward, found it was a far cry back to the lost heights, and wrote the story of his broken life in the song of "the bird with the broken pinion, that never flew as high again." Sooner or later each life passes under bondage. For all strength will vanish as the morning dew our joys take wings and flit away; the eye dim, the ear dull, the thought decay, our dearest die. Oft life's waves and billows chill us to the very marrow, while we gasp and shiver midst the surging tide. Then it is a blessed thing to look out through blinding tears upon a friendly face, to feel the touch of a friendly hand and to know there are some who "remember those in bonds, as bound with them."

Now this principle of social sympathy and liability gives us the secret of all the epoch-making men of our time. Carlyle once called Ruskin "the seer that guides his generation." More recently a prominent philanthropist said: "All our social reform movements are largely the influence of John Ruskin." How earned this man such meed of praise? Upon John Ruskin fortune poured forth all her gifts. He was born the child of supreme genius. He was heir to nearly a million dollars, and by his pen earned a fortune in addition. At the age of 21, when most young men were beginning their reading, he completed a book that put his name and fame in every man's mouth. "For a thousand who can speak, there is but one who can think; for a thousand who can think, there is but one who can see," and to this youth was given the open vision. In the hour of fame the rich and great vied to do him honor, and every door opened at his touch. But he turned aside to become the knight-errant of the poor. Walking along Whitechapel road he saw multitudes of shopmen and shopwomen whose stint was eighty hours a week, who toiled mid poisoned air until the brain reeled, the limbs trembled, and worn out physically and mentally they succumbed to spinal disease or premature age, leaving behind only enfeebled progeny, until the city's streets became graves of the human physique. In that hour London seemed to him like a prison or hospital; nor was it given to him to play upon its floor as some rich men do, knitting its straw into crowns that please; clutching at its dust in the cracks of the floor, to die counting the motes by millions. The youth "remembered men in bonds as bound with them." He tithed himself a tenth, then a third, then a half, and at length used up his fortune in noble service. He founded clubs for workingmen and taught them industry, honor and self-reliance. He bought spinning-wheels and raw flax, and made pauper women self-supporting. He founded the Sheffield Museum, and placed there his paintings and marbles, that workers in iron and steel might have the finest models and bring all their handiwork up toward beauty. He asked his art-students in Oxford to give one hour each day to pounding stones and filling holes in the street. When his health gave way Arnold Toynbee, foreman of his student gang, went forth to carry his lectures on the industrial revolution up and down the land. Falling on hard days and evil tongues and lying customs, he wore himself out in knightly service. So he gained his place among "the immortals." But the secret of his genius and influence is this: He fulfilled the debt of strength and the law of social sympathy and service.

This spirit of sympathetic helpfulness has also given us what is called "the new womanhood." To-day our civilization is rising to higher levels. Woman has brought love into law, justice into institutions, ethics into politics, refinement into the common life. Reforms have become possible that were hitherto impracticable. King Arthur's Knights of the Round Table marching forth for freeing some fair lady were never more soldierly than these who have become the friends and protectors of the poor. The movement began with Mary Ware, who after long absence journeyed homeward. While the coach stopped at Durham she heard of the villages near by where fever was emptying all the homes; and leaving the coach turned aside to nurse these fever-stridden creatures and light them through the dark valley. Then came Florence Nightingale and Mary Stanley, braving rough seas, deadly fever and bitter cold to nurse sick soldiers in Crimea, and returned to find themselves broken in health and slaves to pain, like those whom they remembered. Then rose up a great group of noble women like Mary Lyon and Sarah Judson, who journeyed forth upon errands of mercy into the swamps of Africa and the mountains of Asia, making their ways into garrets and tenements, missionaries of mercy and healing, Knights of the Red Cross and veritable "King's Daughters." No cottage so remote as not to feel this new influence.

Fascinating, also, the life-story of that fair, sweet girl who married Audubon. Yearning for her own home, yet finding that her husband would journey a thousand miles and give months to studying the home and haunts of a bird, she gave up her heart-dreams and went with him into the forest, dwelling now in tents, and now in some rude cabin, being a wanderer upon the face of the earth--until, when children came, she remained behind and dwelt apart. At last the naturalist came home after long absence to fulfill the long-cherished dream of years of quiet study with wife and children, but found that the mice had eaten his drawings and destroyed the sketches he had left behind. Then was he dumb with grief and dazed with pain, but it was his brave wife who led him to the gate and thrust him forth into the forest and sent him out upon his mission, saying that there was no valley so deep nor no wilderness so distant but that his thought, turning homeward, would see the light burning brightly for him. And in those dark days when our land trembled, and a million men from the north tramped southward and a million men from the south tramped northward, and the columns met with a concussion that threatened to rend the land asunder, there, in the battle, midst the din and confusion and blood, women walked, angels of light and mercy, not merely holding the cup of cold water to famished lips, or stanching the life-blood until surgeons came, but teaching soldier boys in the dying hour the way through the valley and beyond it up the heavenly hills. These all fulfilled their mission and "remembered those in bonds as bound with them."

This principle also has been and is the spring of all progress in humanity and civilization. Our journalists and orators pour forth unstinted praise upon the achievements of the nineteenth century. But in what realm lies our supremacy? Not in education, for our schools produce no such thinkers or universal scholars as Plato and his teacher; not in eloquence, for our orators still ponder the periods of the oration "On the Crown;" not in sculpture or architecture, for the broken fragments of Phidias are still models for our youth. The nature of our superiority is suggested when we speak of the doing away with the exposure of children, the building of homes, hospitals and asylums for the poor and weak; the caring for the sick instead of turning them adrift; the support of the aged instead of burying them alive; the diminished frequency of wars; the disappearance of torture in obtaining testimony; humanity toward the shipwrecked, where once luring ships upon the rocks was a trade; the settlement of disputes by umpires and of national differences by arbitration.

Humanity and social sympathy are the glory of our age. Society has come to remember that those in bonds are bound by them. Indeed, the application of this principle to the various departments of human life furnishes the historian with the milestones of human progress. The age of Sophocles was not shocked when the poet wrote the story of the child exposed by the wayside to be adopted by some passer-by, or torn in pieces by wild dogs, or chilled to death in the cold. When the wise men brought their gold and frankincense to the babe in the manger, men felt the sacredness of infancy. As the light from the babe in Correggio's "Holy Night" illumined all the surrounding figures, so the child resting in the Lord's arms for shelter and sacred benediction began to shed luster upon the home and to lead the state. To-day the nurture and culture in the schools are society's attempt to remember the little ones in bonds. Fulfilling the same law Xavier, with his wealth and splendid talents, remembered bound ones and journeyed through India, penetrating all the Eastern lands, being physician for the sick, nurse for the dying, minister for the ignorant; his face benignant; his eloquence, love; his atmosphere, sympathy; carrying his message of peace to the farther-most shores of the Chinese Sea, through his zeal for "those who were in bonds." And thus John Howard visited the prisons of Europe for cleansing these foul dens and wiped from the sword of justice its most polluting stain. Fulfilling the debt of strength, Wilberforce and Garrison, Sumner and Brown, fronted furious slave-holders, enduring every form of abuse and vituperation and personal violence, and destroyed the infamous traffic in human flesh.

This new spirit of sympathy and service it is that offers us help in solving the problems of social unrest and disquietude. Events will not let us forget that ours is an age of industrial discontent. Society is full of warfare. Prophets of evil tidings foretell social revolution. The professional agitators are abroad, sowing discord and nourishing hatred and strife, and even the optimists sorrowfully confess the antagonism between classes. There is an industrial class strong and happy, both rich and poor; and there is an idle class weak and wicked and miserable, among both rich and poor. Unfortunately, as has been said, the wise of one class contemplate only the foolish of the other. The industrious man of means is offended by the idle beggar, and identifies all the poor with him, and the hard-working but poor workman despises the licentious luxury of one rich man, and identifies all the rich with him. But there are idle poor and idle rich and busy poor and busy rich. "If the busy rich people watched and rebuked the idle rich people, all would be well; and if the busy poor people watched and rebuked the idle poor people all would be right. Many a beggar is as lazy as if he had $10,000 a year, and many a man of large fortune is busier than his errand boy."

Forgetting this, some poor look upon the rich as enemies and desire to pillage their property, and some rich have only epithets for the poor. Now, wise men know that there is no separation of rich industrious classes and the poor industrious classes, for they differ only as do two branches of one tree. This year one bough is full of bloom, and the other bears only scantily, but next year the conditions will be reversed. Wealth and poverty are like waves; what is now crest will soon be trough. Such conditions demand forbearance and mutual sympathy. Some men are born with little and some with large skill for acquiring wealth, the two differing as the scythe that gathers a handful of wheat differs from the reaper built for vast harvests and carrying the sickle of success. For generations the ancestors back of one man's father were thrifty and the ancestors back of his mother were far-sighted, and the two columns met in him, and like two armies joined forces for a vast campaign for wealth. Beside him is a brother, whose thoughts and dreams go everywhither with the freedom of an eagle, but who walks midst practical things with the eagle's halting gait. The strong one was born, not for spoiling his weaker brother, but to guard and guide and plan for him.

This is the lesson of nature--the strong must bear the burdens of the weak. To this end were great men born. Nature constantly exhibits this principle. The shell of the peach shelters the inner seed; the outer petals of the bud the tender germ; the breast of the mother-bird protects the helpless birdlets; the eagle flies under her young and gently eases them to the ground; above the babe's helplessness rise the parents' shield and armor. God appoints strong men, the industrial giants, to protect the weak and poor. The laws of helpfulness ask them to forswear a part of their industrial rights; and they fulfill their destiny only by fulfilling the debt of strength to weakness.

To identify one's self with those in bonds is the very core of the Christian life. Not an intellectual belief within, not a form of worship without, but sympathetic helpfulness betokens the true Christian. God, who hath endowed the soul with capacity to endure all labors and pains for wealth, to consume away the very springs of life for knowledge, hath also given it power for pouring itself out in great resistless tides of love and sympathy. For beauty and royal majesty nothing else is comparable to the love of some royal nature. A loving heart exhales sweet odors like an alabaster box; it pours forth joy like a sweet harp; it flashes beauty like a casket of gems; it cheers like a winter's fire; it carries sweet stimulus like returning sunshine. We have all known a few great-hearted men and women who have through years distributed their love-treasures among the little children of the community and scattered affection among the poor and the weak, until the entire community comes to feel that it lives in them and without them will die. Happy the man who hath stored up such treasures of mind and heart as that he stands forth among his fellows like a lighthouse on some ledge, sending guiding rays far out o'er dark and troubled seas. Happy the woman whose ripened affection and inspiration have permeated the common life until to her come the poor and weak and heart-broken, standing forth like some beauteous bower offering shade and filling all the air with sweet perfume.

In crisis hours the patriot and martyr, the hero and the philanthropist, die for the public good, but not less do they serve their fellows who live and through years employ their gifts and heart-treasures, not for themselves, but for the happiness and highest welfare of others. Richter, the German artist, painted a series of paintings illustrating the ministry of angels. He showed us the child-angels who sit talking with mortal children among the flowers, now holding them by their coats lest they fall upon the stairs, now with apples enticing them back when they draw too near the precipice; when the boy grows tall and is tempted, ringing in the chambers of memory the sweet mother's name; in the hour of death coming in the garb of pilgrim, made ready for convoy and guidance to the heavenly land. Oh beautiful pictures! setting forth the sacred ministry of each true Christian heart.

History tells of the servant whose master was sold into Algeria, and who sold himself and wandered years in the great desert in the mere hope of at last finding and freeing his lord; of the obscure man in the Eastern city who, misunderstood and unpopular, left a will stating that he had been poor and suffered for lack of water, and so had starved and slaved through life to build an aqueduct for his native town, that the poor might not suffer as he had; of the soldier in the battle, wounded in cheek and mouth and dying of thirst, but who would not drink lest he should spoil the water for others, and so yielded up his life. But this capacity of sacrifice and sympathy is but the little in man answering to what is large in God. Here deep answers unto deep. The definition of the Divine One is, he remembers those in bonds, and it is more blessed to give than to receive; more blessed to feed the hungry than starving to be fed; more blessed to pour light on darkened misunderstanding than ignorant to be taught; more blessed to open the path through the wilderness of doubt than wandering to be guided; more blessed to bring in the bewildered pilgrim than to be lost and rescued; more blessed to forgive than to be forgiven; to save than to be saved.

# THE TIME ELEMENT IN INDIVIDUAL CHARACTER AND SOCIAL GROWTH.

All that we possess has come to us by way of a long path. There is no instantaneous liberty or wisdom or language or beauty or religion. Old philosophies, old agriculture, old domestic arts, old sciences, medicine, chemistry, astronomy, old modes of travel and commerce, old forms of government and religion have all come in gracefully or ungracefully and have said: 'Progress is king, and long live the king!' Year after year the mind perceives education to expand, art sweeps along from one to ten, music adds to its early richness, love passes outwardly from self towards the race, friendships become laden with more pleasure, truths change into sentiments, sentiments blossom into deeds, nature paints its flowers and leaves with richer tints, literature becomes the more perfect picture of a more perfect intellect, the doctrines of religion become broader and sweeter in their philosophy."--***David Swing***.

For all lovers of their kind, nothing is so hard to bear as the slowness of the upward progress of society. It is not simply that the rise of the common people is accompanied with heavy wastes and losses, it is that the upward movement is along lines so vast as to make society's growth seem tardy, delayed, or even reversed. Doubtless the drift of the ages is upward, but this progress becomes apparent only when age is compared with age and century with century. It is not easy for some Bruno or Wickliffe, sowing the good seed of liberty and toleration in one century, to know that not until another century hath passed will the precious harvest be reaped. Man is accustomed to brief intervals. Not long the space between January's snowdrifts and June's red berries. Brief the interval between the egg and the eagle's full flight. Scarcely a score of years separates the infant of days from the youth of full stature. Trained to expect the April seed to stand close beside the August sheaf, it is not easy for man to accustom himself to the processes of him with whom four-score years are but a handbreadth and a thousand years as but one day.

To man, therefore, toiling upon his industry, his art, his government, his religion, comes this reflection: Because the divine epochs are long, let not the patriot or parent be sick with hope long deferred. Let the reformer sow his seed untroubled when the sickle rusts in the hand that waits for its harvest. Remember that as things go up in value, the period between inception and fruition is protracted. Because the plant is low, the days between seed and sheaf are few and short; because the bird is higher, months stand between egg and eagle. But manhood is a thing so high, culture and character are harvests so rich as to ask years and even ages for ripening, while God's purposes for society involve such treasures of art, wisdom, wealth, law, liberty, as to ask eons and cycles for their full perfection. Therefore let each patriot and sage, each reformer and teacher be patient. The world itself is a seed. Not until ages have passed shall it burst into bloom and blossom.

Troubled by the strifes of society, depressed by the waste of its forces and the delays of its columns, he who seeks character for himself and progress for his kind, oft needs to shelter himself beneath that divine principle called the time-element for the individual and the race. Optimists are we; our world is God's; wastes shall yet become savings and defeats victories; nevertheless, life's woes, wrongs and delays are such as to stir misgiving. The multitudes hunger for power and influence, hunger for wealth and wisdom, for happiness and comfort; satisfaction seems denied them. Watt and Goodyear invent, other men enter into the fruit of their inventions; Erasmus and Melanchthon sow the good seeds of learning; two centuries pass by before God's angels count the bundles. In a passion of enthusiasm for England's poor, Cobden wore his life out toiling for the corn laws. The reformer died for the cotton-spinners as truly as if he had slit his arteries and emptied out the crimson flood. But when the victory was won, the wreath of fame was placed upon another's brow. One day Robert Peel arose in the House of Commons and in the presence of an indignant party and an astounded country, proudly said: "I have been wrong. I now ask Parliament to repeal the law for which I myself have stood. Where there was discontent, I see contentment; where there was turbulence, I see peace, where there was disloyalty, I see loyalty." Then the fury of party anger burst upon him, and bowing to the storm, Robert Peel went forth while men hissed after him such words as "traitor," "coward," "recreant leader." Nor did he foresee that in losing an office he had gained the love of a country.

What delays also in justice! What recognition does society withhold from its heroes! What praise speaks above the pulseless corpse that is denied the living, hungering heart! What gold coin spent for the marble wreath by those who have no copper for laurel for the living hero! How do rewards that dazzle in prospect, in possession, burst like gaudy bubbles! Honors are evanescent; reputation is a vapor; property takes wings; possessions counted firm as adamant dissolve like painted clouds; in the hour of depression the hand drops its tool, the heart its task. In such dark hours and moods, strong men reflect that he who sows the good seed of liberty or culture or character must have long patience until the harvest; that as things go up in value they ask for longer time; that he is the true hero who redeems himself out of present defeat by the foresight of far-off and future victory; that that man has a patent of nobility from God himself who can lay out his life upon the principle that a thousand years are as one day. The truly great man takes long steps by God's side, has the courage of the future; working, he can also wait.

For man, fulfilling such a career, no principle hath greater practical value than this one; as things rise in the scale of value the interval between seedtime and harvest must lengthen. Happily for us, God hath capitalized this principle in nature and life. Each gardener knows that what ripens quickest is of least worth. The mushroom needs only a night; the moss asks a week for covering the fallen tree; the humble vegetable asks several weeks and the strawberry a few months; but, planting his apple tree, the gardener must wait a few years for his ripened russet, and the woodsman many years for the full-grown oak or elm. If in thought we go back to the dawn of creation--to that moment when sun and planet succeeded to clouds of fire, when a red-hot earth, cooling, put on an outer crust, when gravity drew into deep hollows the waters that cooled the earth and purified the upper air--and then follow on in nature's footsteps, passing up the stairway of ascending life from lichen, moss and fern, on to the culminating moment in man, we shall ever find that increase of value means an increase of time for growth. The fern asks days, the reed asks weeks, the bird for months, the beast for a handful of years, but man for an epoch measured by twenty years and more. To grow a sage or a statesman nature asks thirty years with which to build the basis of greatness in the bone and muscle of the peasant grandparents, thirty years in which to compact the nerve and brain of parents; thirty years more in which the heir of these ancestral gifts shall enter into full-orbed power and stand forth fully furnished for his task. Nature makes a dead snowflake in a night, but not a living star-flower. For her best things nature asks long time.

The time-principle holds equally in man's social and industrial life. To-day our colleges have their anthropological departments and our cities their museums. The comparative study of the dress, weapons, tools, houses, ships of savage and civilized races gives an outline view of the progress of society. How fragile and rude the handiwork of savages! How quickly are the wants provided for! A few fig leaves make a full summer suit for the African and the skin of an ox his garb for winter. But civilized man must toil long upon his loom for garments of wool and fine silk. Slowly the hollow log journeys toward the ocean steamer; slowly the forked stick gives place to the steam-plow, the slow ox to the swift engine; slowly the sea-shell, with three strings tied across its mouth, develops into the many-mouthed pipe-organ. But if rude and low conveniences represent little time and toil, these later inventions represent centuries of arduous labor. In his history of the German tribes, Tacitus gives us a picture of a day's toil for one of the forest children. Moving to the banks of some new stream, the rude man peels the bark from the tree and bends it over the tent pole; with a club he beats down the nuts from the branches; with a round stone he knocks the squirrel from the bough; another hour suffices for cutting a line from the ox's hide and, hastily making a hook out of the wishbone of the bird, he draws the trout from its stream. But if for savage man a day suffices for building and provisioning the tent, the accumulated wisdom of centuries is required for the home of to-day. One century offers an arch for the door, another century offers glass windows, another offers wrought nails and hinges, another plaster that will receive and hold the warm colors, another offers the marble, tapestry, picture and piano, the thousand conveniences for use and beauty.

Husbandry also represents patience and the labor of generations. Were it given to the child, tearing open the golden meat of the fruit, to trace the ascent of the tree, he would see the wild apple or bitter orange growing in the edge of the ancient forest.  But man, standing by the fruit, grafted it for sweetness, pruned it for the juicy flow, nourished it for taste and color.  Could he who picks the peach or pear have this inner vision, he would behold an untold company of husbandmen standing beneath the branches and pointing to their special contributions.  The fathers labored, the children entered into the fruitage of the labor in his dream; the poet slept in St. Peter's and saw the shadowy forms of all the architects and builders from the beginning of time standing about him and giving their special contributions to Bramante and Angelo's great temple.  Thus many hands have toiled upon man's house, man's art, industry, invention.

In the realm of law and liberty the best things ask for patience and waiting.  Out of nothing nothing comes.  The institution that represents little toil but little time endures.  Man's early history is involved in obscurity, largely because his early arts were mushroomic--completed quickly, they quickly perished.  The ideas scratched upon the flat leaf or the thin reed represented scant labor and therefore soon were dust.  But he who holds in his hand a modern book holds the fruitage of years many and long.  For that book we see the workmen ranging far for linen; we see the printer toiling upon his movable types; we see the artist etching his plate; the author giving his days to study and his nights to reflection; and because the book harvests the study of a great man's lifetime it endures throughout generations.  The sciences also increase in value only as the time spent upon them is lengthened.  Few and brief were the days required for the early astronomers to work out the theory that the earth is flat, the sky a roof, the stars holes in which the gods have hung lighted lamps.  The theory that makes our earth sweep round the sun, our sun sweep round a far-off star, all lesser groups sweep round one central sun, that shepherds all the other systems, asks for the toil of Galileo and Kepler, of Copernicus and Newton, and a great company of modern students.  The father of astronomy had to wait a thousand years for the fruition of his science.  Upon those words, called law or love, or mother or king, man hath with patience labored.  The word wife or mother is so rich to-day as to make Homer's ideal, Helen, seem poor and almost contemptible.  The girl was very beautiful, but very painful the alacrity with which she passes from the arms of Menelaus to the arms of Paris, from the arms of Paris to those of Deiphobus, his conqueror.  If one hour only was required for this lovely creature to pack her belongings preparatory to moving to the tent of her new lord, one day fully sufficed for transferring her affections from one prince to another. But, toiling ever upward to her physical beauty, woman added mental beauty, moral beauty, until the word wife or mother or home came to have almost infinite wealth of meaning.

In government also the best political instruments ask for longest time. Hercules ruled by the right of physical strength. Assembling the people, he challenged all rivals to combat. A single hour availed for cutting off the head of his enemy. Henceforth he reigned an unchallenged king. Because man hath with patience toiled long upon this republic, how rich and complex its institutions! The modern presidency does not represent the result of an hour's combat between two Samsons. Forty years ago the eager aspirants began their struggle. A great company of young men all over the land determined to build up a reputation for patriotism, statesmanship, wisdom and character. As the time for selecting a president approached, the people passed in review all these leaders. When two or more were finally chosen out, there followed months in which the principles of the candidates were sifted and analyzed. "I know of no more sublime spectacle," said Stuart Mill, "than the election of the ruler under the laws of the republic. If the voice of the people is ever the voice of God, if any ruler rules by divine right, it is when millions of freemen, after long consideration, elect one man to be their appointed guide and leader." If a single hour availed for Samson to settle the question of his sovereignty, free institutions ask for their statesmen to have the patience of years; working, they must also wait.

With long patience also man has worked and waited as he has toiled upon his idea of religion. Rude, indeed, man's hasty thoughts of the infinite. In early days the sun was God's eye, the thunder his voice, the stroke of the earthquake the stroke of his arm, the harvest indicated his pleasure, the pestilence his anger. In such an age the priest and philosopher taxed their genius to invent methods of preserving the friendship and avoiding the anger of the Infinite. Daily the king and general calculated how many sheep and oxen they must slay to avoid defeat in battle. Daily the husbandman and farmer calculated how many doves and lambs must be killed to avert blight from the vineyard and hailstorms from the harvests. Observing that when the king ascended to the throne the slaves put their necks under his heel and covered their bodies with dust, in their haste the priests concluded that by degrading man God would be exalted. Prostrating themselves in dirt and rags, men went down in order that by contrast the throne of God might rise up. The mud was made thick upon man's brow that the crown upon the brow of God might be made brilliant. Out of this degrading thought grew the idea that God lived and ruled for his own gratification and self-glory. The infinite throne was unveiled as a throne of infinite self-aggrandizement. Slowly it was perceived that the parent who makes all things move about himself as a center, ever monopolizing the best food, the best place, the best things, at last becomes a monster of selfishness and suffers an awful degradation, while he who sacrifices himself for others is the true hero.

At last, Christ entered the earthly scene with his golden rule and his new commandment of love. He unveiled God, not as desiring to be ministered to, but as ministering; as being rich, yet for man's sake becoming poor; as asking little, but giving much; as caring for the sparrow and lily; as waiting upon each beetle, bird and beast, and caring for each detail of man's life. Slowly the word God increased in richness. Having found through his telescope worlds so distant as to involve infinite power, man emptied the idea of omnipotence into the word GOD; finding an infinite wisdom in the wealth of the summers and winters, man added the idea of omniscience; noting a certain upward tendency in society, man added the word, "Providence;" gladdened by God's mercy, man added ideas of forgiveness and love. Slowly the word grew. In the olden time people entering the Acropolis cast their gifts of gold and silver into some vase. Last of all came the prince to empty in jewels and flashing gems and make the vase to overflow. Not otherwise Christ emptied vast wealth of meaning into those words called "conscience," "law," "love," "vicarious suffering," "immortality," "God." Beautiful, indeed, the simplicity of Christ. With long patience, man waited for the unveiling of the face of divine love.

To all patriots and Christian men who seek to use occupation and profession so as to promote the world's upward growth comes the reflection that henceforth society's progress must be slow, because its institutions are high and complex. Today many look into the future with shaded eyes of terror. In the social unrest and discontent of our times timid men see the brewing of a social and industrial storm. In their alarm, amateur reformers bring in social panaceas, conceived in haste and born in fear. But God cannot be hurried. His century plants cannot be forced to blossom in a night. No reformer can be too zealous for man's progress, though he can be too impatient. In these days, when civilization has become complex and the fruitage high, those who work must also wait and with patience endure.

Multitudes are abroad trying to settle the labor problem. The labor problem will never be settled until the last man lies in the graveyard. Each new inventor reopens the labor problem. Men were contented with their wages until Gutenberg invented his type and made books possible; then straightway every laborer asked an increased wage, that though he died ignorant his children might be intelligent. When society had readjusted things and man had obtained the larger wage, Arkwright came, inventing his new loom, Goodyear came with the use of rubber, and straightway men asked a new wage to advantage themselves of woolen garments and rubber goods for miners and sailors. On the morrow 15,000,000 children will enter the schoolroom; before noon the teacher has given them a new outlook upon some book, some picture, some convenience, some custom. Each child registers the purpose to go home immediately and cry to his parent for that book or picture; that tool or comfort. When the parents return that night the labor question has been reopened in millions of homes.

Intelligence is emancipating man. Ignorance is a constant invitation to oppression. So long as workmen are ignorant, governments will oppress them; wealth will oppress them; religious machinery will oppress them. Education can make man's wrists too large to be holden of fetters. In the autumn the forest trees tighten the bark, but when April sap runs through the trees the trunk swells, the bark is strained and despite all protests it splits and cracks. The splitting of the bark saves the life of the tree. The soft, balmy air of April is passing over the world and succeeding to the winter of man's discontent. Old ideas are being rent asunder and old institutions are being succeeded by new ones. God is abroad destroying that he may save. In every age he makes the discontent of the present to be the prophecy of the higher civilization. Despite all the pessimists and the croakers, the ideas of manhood were never so high as to-day, and the number of those whose hearts are knitted in with their kind was never so large nor so noble. The movement may be slow, but it is because the social organs are complex and intricate. With long patience man must work and also wait.

In the world of business, also, the time element exerts striking influence. To-day our land is filled with men who have sown the seed of thought and purpose, but whose harvest is of so high a quality that with long patience must they wait for the fruition. How pathetic the reverses of the last four years. The condition of our land as to the overthrows of its leaders answers to the condition in Poland when Kossuth and his fellow patriots, accustomed to life's comforts and its luxuries, went forth penniless exiles to accustom themselves to menial toil, to hardship and extreme poverty. His heart must be of iron who can behold those who have been leaders of the industrial column, who now stand aside and see the multitude sweep by. Just at the moment of expected victory misfortune overtook them and brought their structure down in ruins. And because the seed they have sown is not physical, but mental and moral, the fruition is long postponed.

Walter Scott tells the story of a wounded knight, who took refuge in the castle of a baron that proved to be a secret enemy and threw the knight into a dungeon; one day in his cell the knight heard the sound of distant music approaching. Drawing near the slit in the tower, he saw the flash of swords and heard the tramp of marching men. At last the wounded hero realized that these were his own troops, marching by in ignorance of the fact that the lord of this castle was also the jailer of their general. While the knight tugged at his chain, lifted up his voice and cried aloud, his troops marched on, their music drowning out his cries. Soon the banners passed from sight, the last straggler disappeared behind the hill and the captive was left alone. The brave knight died in his dungeon, but the story of his heroism lived. What the knight learned in suffering the poets have taught in song. The captive hero has a permanent place in civilization, though the foresight of his influence was denied him.

Those whose harvest is delayed are a great company. Elizabeth Barrett Browning exclaiming, "I have not used half the powers God has given me," poets dying ere the day was half done; the inventors and reformers denied their ideals; obscure and humble workmen--the mechanic who emancipates man by his machine; the artisan whose conveniences are endless benefactions to our homes; the smith whose honest anchor holds the ship in time of storm--all these labored and died without seeing the fruitage, but other men entered into their labors.

To parents who have passed through all the thunder of life's battle and stand at the close of life's day discouraged because children are unripe, thoughtless and immature; to publicists and teachers, sowing God's precious seed, but denied its harvests; to individuals seeking to perfect their character within themselves comes this thought--that character is a harvest so rich as to ask for long waiting and the courage of far-off results. Nature can perfect physical processes in twenty years, but long time is asked for teaching the arm skill, the tongue its grace of speech, to clothe reason with sweetness and light, to cast error out of the judgment, to teach the will hardness and the heart hope and endurance.

Four hundred years passed by before the capstone was placed upon the Cathedral of Cologne, but no trouble requires such patient toil as the structure of manhood. For complexity and beauty nothing is comparable to character. Great artists spend years upon a single picture. With a touch here and a touch there they approach it, and when a long period hath passed they bring it to completion. Yet all the beauty of paintings, all the grace of statues, all the grandeur of cathedrals are as nothing compared to the painting of that inner picture, the chiseling of that inner manhood, the adornment of that inner temple, that is scarcely begun when the physical life ends. How majestic the full disclosure of an ideal manhood! With what patience must man wait for its completion! Here lies the hope of immortality; it does not yet appear what man shall be.

# THE SUPREMACY OF HEART OVER BRAIN.

"Out of the heart are the issues of life."--*Prov. IV. 23*.

"For out of the heart man believeth unto righteousness."--*Paul*.

"Heart is a word that the Bible is full of. Brain, I believe, is not mentioned in Scripture. Heart, in the sense in which it is currently understood, suggests the warm center of human life or any other life. When we say of a man that he 'has a good deal of heart' we mean that he is 'summery.' When you come near him it is like getting around to the south side of a house in midwinter and letting the sunshine feel of you, and watching the snow slide off the twigs and the tear-drops swell on the points of pendant icicles. Brain counts for a good deal more to-day than heart does. It will win more applause and earn a larger salary. Thought is driven with a curb-bit lest it quicken into a pace and widen out into a swing that transcends the dictates of good form. Exuberance is in bad odor. Appeals to the heart are not thought to be quite in good taste. The current demand is for ideas--not taste. I asked a member of my church the other day whether he thought a certain friend of his who attends a certain church and is exceptionally brainy was really entering into sympathy with religious things. 'Oh, no,' he said, 'he likes to hear preaching because he has an active mind, and the way that things are spread out in front of him.' In the old days of the church a sermon used to convert 3,000 men, now that temperature is down it takes 3,000 sermons to convert one man."--*Charles H. Parkhurst*.

To-day there has sprung up a rivalry between brain and heart. Men are coming to idolize intellect. Brilliancy is placed before goodness and intellectual dexterity above fidelity. Intellect walks the earth a crowned king, while affection and senti-ment toil as bond slaves. Doubtless our scholars, with the natural bias for their own class, are largely responsible for this worship of intellectuality. When the historian calls the roll of earth's favorite sons he causes these immortals to stand forth an army of great thinkers, including philosophers, scientists, poets, jurists, generals. The great minds are exalted, the great hearts are neglected.

Artists also have united with authors for strengthening this idolatry of intel-lect. One of the great pictures in the French Academy of Design assembles the im-mortals of all ages. Having erected a tribunal in the center of the scene, Delaroche places Intellect upon the throne. Also, when the sons of genius are assembled about that glowing center, all are seen to be great thinkers. There stand Democritus, a thinker about invisible atoms; Euclid, a thinker about invisible lines and angles; Newton, a thinker about an invisible force named gravity; La Place, a thinker about the invisible law that sweeps suns and stars forward toward an unseen goal.

The artist also remembers the inventors whose useful thoughts blossom into engines and ships; statesmen whose wise thoughts blossom into codes and constitu-tions; speakers whose true thoughts blossom into orations, and artists whose beau-tiful thoughts appear as pictures. At this assembly of the immortals great thinkers touch and jostle. But if the great minds are remembered, no chair is made ready for the great hearts. He who lingers long before this painting will believe that brain is king of the world; that great thinkers are the sole architects of civilization; that science is the only providence for the future; that God himself is simply an infinite brain, an eternal logic engine, cold as steel, weaving endless ideas about life and art, about nature and man.

But the throne of the universe is mercy and not marble; the name of the world-ruler is Great Heart, rather than Crystalline Mind, and God is the Eternal Friend who pulsates out through his world those forms of love called reforms, philanthro-pies, social bounties and benefactions, even as the ocean pulsates its life-giving tides into every bay and creek and river. The springs of civilization are not in the mind. For the individual and the state, "out of the heart are the issues of life."

What intellect can dream, only the heart realizes! John Cabot's mind did, in-deed, blaze a pathway through the New England forest. But with burning hearts and iron will the Pilgrim Fathers loved liberty, law and learning, and soon they broadened the path into a highway for commerce, turned tepees into temples and made the forests a land of vineyards and villages. Mind is the beginning of civilization, but the ends and fruitage thereof are of the heart.

Christopher Wren's intellect wrought out the plan for St. Paul's Cathedral. But all impotent to realize themselves, these plans, lying in the King's council chamber grew yellow with age and thick with dust. One day a great heart stood forth before the people of London, pointing them to an unseen God, "from whom cometh every good and perfect gift," and, plying men with the generosity of God, he asked gifts of gold and silver and houses and lands, that England might erect a temple worthy of him "whom the heaven of heavens could not contain." The mind of a great architect had created a plan and a "blue-print," but eager hearts inspiring earnest hands turned the plan into granite and hung in the air a dome of marble.

Thus all the great achievements for civilization are the achievements of heart. What we call the fine arts are only red-hot ingots of passion cooled off into visible shape. All high music is emotion gushing forth at those faucets named musical notes. As unseen vapors cool into those visible forms named snowflakes, so Gothic enthusiasms cooled off into cathedrals.

Our art critics speak of the eight great paintings of history. Each of these masterpieces does but represent a holy passion flung forth upon a canvas. The reformation also was not achieved by intellect nor scholarship. Erasmus represents pure mind. Yet his intellect was cold as winter sunshine that falls upon a snowdrift and dazzles the eyes with brightness, yet is impotent to unlock the streams, or bore a hole through the snowdrifts, or release the roots from the grip of ice and frost, or cover the land with waving harvests. Powerless as winter sunshine were Erasmus' thoughts. But what the scholar could not do, Luther, the great heart, wrought easily.

Thus all the reforms represent passions and enthusiasms. That citadel called "The Divine Right of Kings" was not overthrown by colleges with books and pamphlets. It was the pulse-beats of the heart of the people that pounded down the Bastille. Ideas of the iniquity of slavery floated through our land for three centuries, yet the slave pen and auction block still cursed our land. At last an enthusiasm for man as man and a great passion for the poor stood behind these ideas of human brotherhood, and as powder stands behind the bullet, flinging forth its weapons, slavery perished before the onslaught of the heart.

The men whose duty it was to follow the line of battle and bury our dead soldiers tell us that in the dying hour the soldier's hand unclasped his weapon and reached for the inner pocket to touch some faded letter; some little keepsake, some likeness of wife or mother. This pathetic fact tells us that soldiers have won their battles not by holding before the mind some abstract thought about the rights of man. The philosopher did, indeed, teach the theory, and the general marked out the line of attack or defense, but it was love of home and God and native land that entered into the soldier and made his arm invincible. Back of the emancipation proclamation stands a great heart named Lincoln. Back of Africa's new life stands a great heart named Livingstone. Back of the Sermon on the Mount stands earth's greatest heart--man's Savior. Christ's truth is enlightening man's ignorance, but his tears, falling upon our earth, are washing away man's sin and woe.

Impotent the intellect without the support of the heart. How thickly are the shores of time strewn with those forms of wreckage called great thoughts. In those far-off days when the overseers of the Egyptian King scourged 80,000 slaves forth to their task of building a pyramid, a great mind discovered the use of steam. Intellect achieved an instrument for lifting blocks of granite into proper place. In that hour thought made possible the freedom of innumerable slaves. But the heart of the tyrant held no love for his bondsmen. The poor seemed of less worth than cattle. Because the King's heart felt no woes to be cured, his hand pushed away the engine. A great thought was there, but not the kindly impulse to use it. Then, full 2,000 years passed over our earth. At last came an era when man's heart journeyed forward with his mind. Then the woes of miners and the world's burden-bearers filled the ears of James Watt with torment, and his sympathetic heart would not let him stay until he had fashioned his redemptive tool.

For generations, also, the thoughts of liberty waited for the heart to re-enforce them and make them practical in institutions. Two thousand years before the era of Cromwell and Hampden, Grecian philosophers wrought out a full statement for the republic and individual liberty. The right of life and liberty and the pursuit of happiness were truths clearly perceived by Plato and Pericles. But the heart loved luxury and soft, silken refinements, and Grecian philosophers in their palaces refused to let their slaves go.

Wide, indeed, the gulf separating our age of kindness from Cicero's age of cruelty! The difference is almost wholly a difference of heart. This age has oratory and wisdom, and so had Cicero's; this age has poetry and art, and so had that; but our age has heart and sympathy, and Cicero's had not. Caesar's mind was the mind of a scholar, but his hands were red with the blood of a half-million men slain in unjust wars. Augustus loved refinement, literature and music. He assembled at his table the scholars of a nation, yet his culture did not forbid the slaying of ten thousand gladiators at his various garden parties.

We admire Pliny's literary style. One evening Pliny returned home from the funeral of the wife of a friend and sat down to write that friend a note of gratitude for having so arranged the gladiatorial spectacle as to make the funeral service pass off quite pleasantly. For that age of intellect was also an age of blood; the era of art and luxury was also an era of cruelty and crime. The intellect lent a shining luster to the era of Augustus, but because it was intellect only it was gilt and not gold. Had the heart re-enforced the intellect with sympathy and justice the age of Augustus might have been an era golden, indeed, and also perpetual.

Great men capitalize the impotency of unsupported intellect. Ten-talent men have often known more than they would do. The children of genius have not always lived up to their moral light. Burns' mind ran swiftly forward, but his will followed afar off. If the poet's forehead was in the clouds, his feet were in the mire. How noble, also, Byron's thoughts, but how mean his life! Goethe uttered the wisdom of a sage, as did Rousseau, yet their deeds were often those we would expect from a slave with a low brow. Even of Shakespeare, it is said in the morning he polished his sonnets, while at midnight he poached game from a neighboring estate. Our era bestows unstinted admiration upon the essays of Lord Bacon. How noble his aphorisms! How petty his envy and avarice! What scholarship was his, and what cunning also! With what splendor of argument does he plead for the advancement of learning and liberty! With what meanness does he take bribes from the rich against the poor! His mind seems like a palace of marble with splendid galleries and library and banqueting hall, yet in this palace the spider spins its web and vermin make the foundations to be a noisome place.

In all ages also the intellect of the common people has discerned truth and light that the will has refused to fulfill. Generations ago society discovered the doctrine of industry and integrity, and yet thousands of individuals still prefer to steal or beg or starve rather than work. For centuries the work of moralists and public instructors has not been so much the making known new truth as the inspiring men to do a truth already known. As of old, so now, the word is nigh man, even in his mouth, for enabling society to lift every social burden, right every social wrong, turn each rookery into a house, make each place wealth, make every home happiness, make every child a scholar, a patriot and a Christian. In Solomon's day wisdom stood in the corner of the streets but man would not regard, and the city perished. Should the heart now join the intellect, man's feet would swiftly find these paths that lead to prosperity and perfect peace.

Fascinating, indeed, the question how feeling and sentiment control conduct and character. Modern machinery has thrown light upon the problems of the soul. The engineer finds that his locomotive will not run itself, but waits for the steam to pound upon the piston. The great ships also are becalmed until the trade winds come to beat upon the sails. Informed by these physical facts, we now see a noble thought or ambition or social ideal is a mechanism that will not work itself, but asks the enthusiastic heart to lend power divine. Some of earth's greatest orators, like Patrick Henry, have been unlearned men, but no orator has ever fallen short of being an enthusiastic man. A generation ago there appeared in Paris one whose voice was counted the most perfect voice in Europe. Musical critics gave unstinted praise to the purity of tone and accuracy of execution. Yet in a few weeks the audiences had dwindled to a handful, and in a few years the singer's name was forgotten. Obscurity overtook the singer because there was no heart behind the voice and so the tones became metallic. Contrariwise, the history of Jenny Lind contains a letter to a friend in Sweden, in which the singer writes: "Oh, that I may live two years longer and be permitted to save enough money to complete my orphans' home!" As the sun's warm beams lend a soft blush to the rose and pulsate the crimson tides through to the uttermost edge of each petal, so a great, loving sympathy, sang and sighed, thrilled and throbbed through the tones of the Swedish singer, and ravished the hearts of the people and made her name immortal.

History portrays many men of giant minds whose intellect could not redeem them from aimlessness and obscurity. Not until some divine enthusiasm descended upon the mind and baptized it with heroic action did these men find themselves.

To that young patrician, Saul, journeying to Damascus, came the heavenly vision, and the new impulse of the heart made his cold mind warm, lent wings to his slow feet, made all his days powerful, made his soul the center of an immense activity. This glowing heart of Paul explains for us the fact that he achieved freedom of thought and speech, endured the stones with which he was bruised, the stocks in which he was bound, the mobbings with which he was mutilated; explains also his eloquence, known and unrecorded; explains his faith and fortitude, his heroism in death. And not only has the zeal of the heart made strong men stronger, turned weak men into giants, lent the soldier his conquering courage and lent the scholar a stainless life--to men whose will has been made weak by indulgence, the new love has come to redeem intellect and will from the bondage of habit.

No one who ever heard John B. Gough can forget his marvelous eloquence, his wit and his pathos, his scintillating humor, his inimitable dramatisms. He did not have the polished brilliancy of Everett or the elegant scholarship of Phillips, and yet when these numbered thousands of admirers, Gough numbered his tens of thousands. In his autobiography this man tells us to what sad straits passion had brought him; how he reflected upon the injury he was doing himself and others, only to find that his reflections and resolutions snapped like cobwebs before the onslaught of temptation. One night the young bookbinder drifted into a little meeting and, buttoning his seedy overcoat to conceal his rags, in some way he found himself upon his feet and began to speak. The address that proved a pleasure to others was a revelation to himself. For the first time Gough tasted the joys of moving men and mastering them for good. Within a week that love of public speech and useful service had kindled his mental faculties into a creative glow. The new and higher love of the heart consumed the lower love of the body, just as the sun melts manacles of ice from a man's wrist.

History is full of these transformations wrought by the heart. It was a new enthusiasm that changed Augustine the epicurean into Augustine the church father. It was a new enthusiasm that turned Howard the pleasure-lover into Howard the prison-reformer. It was a glowing heart that lent power to Mazzini and Garibaldi and gave Italy her new hope and liberty. Indeed, the history of each life is the history of its new loves. The enthusiasms are beacon lights that glow in the highway along which the soul journeys forward. When the hero's ships were becalmed Virgil tells us that Aeolus struck the hollow mountain with his staff and straightway, released from their caves, the winds went forth to stir the waves and smite upon the sails and sweep the becalmed ship on toward its harbor. Oh, beautiful story, telling us how Christ touches the heart with his regenerating hand to release the soul's deeper convictions, to sweep man forward to the heavenly haven!

If sentiment working in sound can make music; if working in colors, etc., it can fill galleries with statues and pictures; if sentiment working in literature can produce poems, it should not seem strange that the heart, with its affections, furnishes the key of knowledge and wisdom. The time was when authors were supposed to think out their truths; now we know that the greatest truths are felt out. Matthew Arnold said that mere knowledge is cold as an icicle, but once experienced and touched with noble feelings truth becomes sweetness and light. This author thought that the first requisite for a good writer was a sensitive and sympathetic heart.

Even in Shakespeare the springs of genius were not in the mind. The heart of our greatest poet was so sensitive that he could not see an apple blossom without hoping that no untimely frost would nip it; could not see the clusters turn purple under the autumn sun without hoping that hailstones would not pound off the rich clusters; could not see a youth leave his home to seek his fortune without praying that he would return to his mother laden with rich treasures; could not see a bride go down the aisle of the church without sending up a petition that many years might intervene before death's hand should touch her white brow. Sympathy in the heart so fed the springs of thought in the mind that it was easy for the poet to put himself in another's place. And so, while his pen wrote, his heart felt itself to be the king and also his servant, to be the merchant and also his clerk, to be the general and also his soldier. He saw the assassin drawing near the throne with a dagger beneath his cloak; he went forth with King Lear to shiver beneath the wintry blasts; he rejoiced with Rosalind and wept with Hamlet, and there was no joy or grief or woe or wrong that ever touched a human heart that he did not perfectly feel and, therefore, perfectly describe. For depth of mind begins with depth of heart. The greatest writers are primarily seers and only incidentally thinkers. As of old, so now, for a thousand thinkers there is only one great seer.

Having affirmed the influence of the heart upon the intellect and scholarship, let us hasten to confess that the heart determines the religious belief and creed. It is often said that belief is a matter of pure reason determined wholly by evidence. And doubtless it is true that in approaching mathematical proofs man is to discharge his mind of all color. That two and two are four is true for the poet and the miser, for the peaceable man not less than the litigious. But of the other truths of life it is a fact that with the heart man believes. We approach wheat with scales, we measure silk with a yardstick; we test the painting with taste and imagination, and the symphony with the sense of melody; motives and actions are tested by conscience; we approach the stars with a telescope, while purity of heart is the glass by which we see God. The scales that are useful in the laboratory are utterly valueless in the art gallery. The scientific faculty that fits Spencer for studying nature unfits him for studying art. In his old age Huxley, the scientist, wrote an essay forty pages long to prove that man was more beautiful than woman. Imagine some Tyndall approaching the transfiguration of Raphael to scrape off the colors and test them with acid and alkali for finding out the proportion of blue and crimson and gold. These are the methods that would give the village paint-grinder precedency above genius itself.

In 1837 two boys entered Faneuil hall and heard Wendell Phillips' defense of Lovejoy. One youth was an English visitor who saw the portraits of Otis and Hancock, yet saw them not; heard the words of Phillips, yet heard them not, and because his heart was in London believed not unto patriotism. But the blood of Adams was in the veins of the other youth. He thought of Samuel Adams, who heard the firing at Lexington and exclaimed; "What a glorious morning this is!" He thought of John Adams and his love of liberty. He thought of the old man eloquent, John Quincy Adams, in the Halls of Congress, and as he listened to the burning words of the speaker, tears filled his eyes and pride filled his soul. It was his native land. With his heart he believed unto patriotism.

What the man is determines largely what his intellect thinks about God. When the heart is narrow, harsh, and rigorous its theology is despotic and cruel. When the heart grows kindly, sympathetic and of autumnal richness, it emphasizes the sympathy and love of God. Each man paints his own picture of God. The heart lends the pigments. Souls full of sweetness and light fill the divine portrait with the lineaments of love. For with the heart man believeth unto righteousness.

Happy, indeed, our age, in that the heart is now beginning to color our civilization. Vast, indeed, the influence of library and lecture-hall, of gallery and store and market-place, but the most significant fact of our day is that sympathy is baptizing our industries and institutions with new effort. Intellect has lent the modern youth instruments many and powerful. Inventive thought has lent fire to man's forge, tools for his hands, books for his reading, has lent arts, sciences, institutions. The modern youth stands forth in the aspect of the Roman conqueror to whom the citizens went forth to bestow gifts, one taking his chariot, one leading a steed, the children scattering flowers in the way, young men and maidens taking the hero's name upon their lips. Unfortunately multitudes have declined those high gifts, turning away from the open door of the schoolhouse and college; many young feet have crossed the threshold of the saloon. Having entered our museum or art-gallery, multitudes enter places of evil resort.

Despising the opportunity offered by music or eloquence, by book or newspaper, by trade and profession, many choose sloth and self-indulgence. These needy millions, blinded with sin and ignorance, stand forth as a great opportunity for loving hearts. Sympathy is making beautiful the pathway of knowledge, that young hearts may be allured along the shining way. By a thousand arts and devices young people of refinement and culture are founding centers of light among the poor. The opportunity that William the Silent found in the starving millions of Holland; that Garrison found in the miserable slaves of the South; that Livingstone found in Africa, the modern hero is finding in the tenement-house district. Through sympathy a new hope is entering into all classes of society.

The heart is also coloring industry. This year it is said that more than a score of great industrial institutions in our country have, to the factory, added gymnasium, recreation-hall, schoolroom, library, free musicals and lectures. The intellect has failed to solve the social problems by giving allopathic doses from Poor Richard's Almanac. Impotent also those dreamers who have insisted that society must have socialism--either God's or the devil's. Impotent those who, during the past week, have proposed to cure economic ills by spitting the heads of tyrants upon bayonets. But what force and law cannot do is slowly being done by sympathy and good-will. The heart is taking the rigor out of toil, the drudgery out of service, the cruelty out of laws, harshness out of theology, injustice out of politics. Love has done much.

The social gains of the future are to be to the gradual progress of sympathy and love.

Unto man who goes through life working, weeping, laughing, loving, comes the heart believing unto immortality. For reason oft the immortal hope burns low and the stars dim and disappear, but for the heart, never! Scientists tell us matter is indestructible. And the heart nourishes an immortal hope that no doubt can quench, no argument destroy, no misfortune annihilate. Comforting, indeed, for reasons, the arguments of Socrates that life survives death. After the death of his beloved daughter Tullia, Cicero outlined arguments which have consoled the mind of multitudes. But in the hour of darkness and blackness, for a man to put out upon Death's dark sea, upon the argument of Cicero, is like some Columbus committing himself to a single plank in the hope of discovering an unseen continent.

In these dark hours the heart speaks. In the poet's vision, to blind Homer, falling into the bog, torn by the thorns and thickets and lost in the forest and the night, came the young goddess, the daughter of Light and Beauty, to take the sightless poet by the hand and lead him up the heavenly heights. Sometimes intellect seems sightless and wanders lost in the maze. Then comes the heart to lead man along the upward path. For even in its dreams the heart hears the sound of invisible music. Oft before reason's eye the heart unveils the Vision Splendid. The soul is big with immortality. When the heart speaks it is God within making overtures for man to come upward toward home and heaven.

# RENOWN THROUGH SELF-RENUNCIATION.

"To live absolutely each man for himself could not be possible if all were to live together.  In course of time, in addition to utility, certain more sensitive individuals began to see a charm, a beauty in this consideration for others.  Gradually a sort of sanctity attached to it, and nature had once more illustrated her mysterious method of evolving from rough and even savage necessities her lovely shapes and her tender dreams.  To assert, then, with some recent critics of Christianity, that that law of brotherly love which is its central teaching is impracticable of application to the needs of society, is simply to deny the very first law by which society exists."--***Richard Le Galliene, in "The Religion of a Literary Man."***

"It is only with renunciations that life, properly speaking, can be said to begin. . . .  In a valiant suffering for others, not in a slothful making others suffer for us, did nobleness ever lie."--***Carlyle***.

"You talk of self as the motive to exertion.  I tell you it is the abnegation of self which has wrought out all that is noble, all that is good, all that is useful, nearly all that is ornamental in the world."--***Whyte Melville***.

"Jesus said; 'Whosoever will come after Me, let him renounce himself, and take up his cross daily and follow Me.'  Perhaps there is no other maxim of Jesus which has such a combined stress of evidence for it and may be taken as so eminently His."--Matthew Arnold.

History has crowned self-sacrifice as one of the virtues.  In all ages selfishness has been like a flame consuming society, like a sword working waste and ruin, but self-sacrifice has repaired these ravages and achieved for man victories many and great. The church owes so much to the company of martyrs whose blood has crimsoned her every page, the state is so deeply indebted to the patriots who have given their lives for liberty, man has derived such strength from those who have endured the fetter and the fagot rather than belie their convictions, woman has derived such beauty from the example of that Antigone who died rather than desert the body of her dead brother, as that each modern youth beholds self-sacrifice standing forth clothed with immeasurable excellence.

Not large the company of the Immortals whose birthdays society celebrates. Yet when on these high days, through song or story the poet or orator draws back the veil and reveals to the assembled multitude the face of some Garibaldi or Hampden or Lincoln, the beloved one is seen to be clothed with genius and beauty and truth indeed, but also to be crowned with self-sacrifice. Society makes haste to forget him who remembers only himself. As there can be no illiterate sage, no ignorant Shakespeare, so history knows no selfish hero. For the mercenary forehead memory has no wreath. A sentinel with a flaming sword guards the threshold of the temple of fame against those aspirants named Ease, Avarice, Self-indulgence.

"Shall I be remembered by posterity?" asked the dying Garfield. In this eager, tremulous question the renowned and the obscure alike have a pathetic interest. For the deeply reflective mind oblivion is a thought all unendurable. The tool man fashions, the structure he rears, the success he achieves, not less than his marble monument, looks down upon the beholder with a mute appeal for recollection. To each eager aspirant for everlasting remembrance Christ comes whispering his secret of abiding renown. Speaking not as an amateur, but as a master, Christ affirms that he who would save his life must lose it, that he who would be remembered by others must forget himself, that the soldier who flees from danger to save his body shall leave that life upon the battlefield, while he who plunges his banner into the very thick of the fight and is carried off the field upon his shield shall in safety bear his life away. Hard seem the terms; they rebuke ease, they smite self-indulgence, they deny the maxims of the worldly wise. But in accepting Christ's principle and forsaking their palaces that they might be as brothers to beggars, Xavier and Loyola found an exhilaration denied to kings; while each Sir Launfal, in his ease denied the Holy Grail, has in the hour of self-sacrifice discerned the Vision Splendid. To each young patriot and soldier looking eagerly unto the tablets that commemorate the deeds of heroes, to each young scholar aspiring to a place beside the sages, comes this word: Life is through death, and immortal renown through self-renunciation.

This law of self-sacrifice is imbedded in nature. Minot, the embryologist, and Drummond, the scientist, tells us that only by losing its life does the cell save it. The new science exhibits the body as a temple, constructed out of cells, as a building is made of bricks. Just as some St. Peter represents strange marble from Athens, beauteous woods from Cyprus, granite from Italy, porphyry from Egypt, all brought together in a single cathedral, so the human body is a glorious temple built by those architects called living cells. When the scientist searches out the beginning of bird or bud or acorn he comes to a single cell. Under the microscope that cell is seen to be absorbing nutrition through its outer covering. But when the cell has attained a certain size its life is suddenly threatened. The center of the cell is seen to be so far from the surface that it can no longer draw in the nutrition from without. The bulk has outrun the absorbing surface. "The alternative is very sharp," says the scientist, "the cell must divide or die." Only by losing its life and becoming two cells can it save its life.

Later on, when each of the two cells has grown again to the size of the original one, the same peril threatens them and they too must divide or die. And when through this law of saving life by losing it nature has made sure the basis for bud and bird, for beast and man, then the principle of sacrifice goes on to secure beauty of the individual plant or animal and perpetuity for the species. In the center of each grain of wheat there is a golden spot that gives a yellow cast to the fine flour. That spot is called the germ. When the germ sprouts and begins to increase, the white flour taken up as food begins to decrease. As the plant waxes, the surrounding kernel wanes. The life of the higher means the death of the lower. In the orchard also the flower must fall that the fruit may swell. If the young apple grows large, it must begin by pushing off the blossom. But by losing the lower bud, the tree saves the higher fruit.

Centuries ago Herodotus, the Grecian traveler, noted a remarkable custom in Egypt. Each springtime, when the palms flowered, the Egyptians went into the desert, cut off branches from the wild palms and, bringing them back to their gardens, waved them over the flowers of the date trees. What was meant by this ceremony

Herodotus did not know. The husbandmen believed that if they neglected it the gods would give them but a scanty crop of dates. It was reserved for the science of our century, through Drummond, to explain the fact that the one palm saved its dates because the other palm lost its fertilizing pollen. Should nature refuse to obey this law of losing life in order to save it, man's world would become one vast Sahara waste, an arctic desolation.

The law of sacrifice is also industrial law. Great is the power of wealth. It buys comfort, it purchases travel, it secures instruments of culture for reason and taste, it is almoner of bounty for sympathy and kindness. Flowing through man's life, it seems like unto some Nile flowing through Egypt with soft, irrigating flow, bearing man's burdens upon its currents, giving food to bird and beast. But the story of each Peter Cooper, each Peabody, each Amos Lawrence, is the story of the ease of life lost to-day that the strength of life may be saved to-morrow. Each young merchant loved luxury and beauty, but in the interests of thrift he denied the eye its hunger, the taste its satisfaction. When pride asked for dress and show, the youth rebuked his vanity. When companions scoffed at the young merchant as a niggard he subdued his sensitiveness and inured himself to rigid economy. When increasing wealth began to lend influence, and society urged him to give his evenings to gayety, the young merchant denied the social instinct and gave his long winter evenings to broadening his knowledge and culture. Having lost the lower good, at last the time came when the American merchant and philanthropist had saved for himself universal fame. Having lost ease and self-indulgence during the first half of his life, he saved the higher ease and comfort for the second period of his career.

Similarly of the young men in Parliament who to-day have charge of the destinies of the English empire, it may be said that they have saved their lives, because the fathers lost theirs. One hundred years ago these fathers made exiles of themselves in the interests of their sons and daughters. The East India merchant exiled himself into the tropic land where heat and malaria made his skin as yellow as the gold he gained. Others braved the perils of the African forests, dared the dangers of Australian deserts, endured the rigor of the arctic cold. Losing the lower and present happiness, they saved the higher ease and comfort for their sons. The self-denial of yesterday brought the influence of to-day. Upon this principle God has organized the industrial world. Man must take his choice between ease and wealth, either may be his but not both.

Sacrifice is also the secret of beauty, culture and character. Selfishness eats sweetness from the singer's voice as rust eats the edge of a sword. St. Cecilia refused to lend the divine touch to lips steeped in pleasure. He who sings for love of gold finds his voice becoming metallic. In art, also, Hitchcock has said: "When the brush grows voluptuous it falls like an angel from heaven." Fra Angelico refuses an invitation to the Pitti palace, choosing rather his crust and pallet in the cell of the monastery. The artist gave his mornings to the poor, his evenings to his canvas. But when the painter had worn his life away in kindly deeds, men found that the light divine had been transferred to the painter's canvas. Eloquence also loves sincere lips. The history of oratory includes few great scenes--Demosthenes' plea for Athenian liberty that resulted in his death, Luther's single challenge to the hosts of Pope and Emperor, Wendell Phillips' at Faneuil Hall, Lincoln's at Gettysburg. All these risked life for a cause, and were baptized with eloquence, their words being tipped with fire, their minds hurling thunderbolts.

Sacrifice also is the secret of beauty. After a little time the life of pleasure and selfishness will make the sweetest fact opaque and repellent, while self-sacrificing thoughts are cosmetics that at last make the plainest face to be beautiful. In the calm of scholarship men have given up the thought that culture consists of an exquisite refinement in manners and dress, in language and equipage. The poet laureate makes Maud the type of polished perfection. She is "icily regular, splendidly null," for culture is more of the heart than of the mind. But as eloquence means that an orator has so mastered the laws of posture, and gesture and thought and speech that they are utterly forgotten, and have become second nature, so knowledge becomes culture, and physical perfection becomes beauty, only when it is unconscious.

In the moral realm also, the gains for the soul begin with loss. In the hour of temptation he who sacrifices the higher duty to the lower pleasure will find that ease has shorn away the strength of Samson.

Victor Hugo has pictured a man committing suicide through poverty, and deserting the duty and dwelling where God has placed him. But waking in the next world, the man perceives a letter on the way to himself announcing a large inheritance which would have been his had he but been patient. Therefore the great novelist affirms that God makes such a man begin over again, only under harder conditions, the existence that here he has willfully shattered. What a tragedy is his who, to save the present good, will lose the higher life. Whittier expressed the fear that Daniel Webster saved his life only to lose it. In his works the poet recalls the time when for genius of statesmanship and weight of mentality Webster's like was not upon our earth. But in an evil hour the statesman saw that the presidency was a prize that could be gained by giving the fugitive slave law as a sop to the South. In that hour his character suffered grievous injury. In the attempt to save men's votes he lost men's higher respect. In deepest sorrow his admirers, abroad and at home, cried out: "O, Lucifer, thou son of the morning, how art thou fallen!"

The law of sacrifice is also the law of progress and civilization. When history exhibits as dead the nations that have been pleasure-seekers it declares that the state that saveth its life shall lose it. In our own land the bankruptcy and gloom that have for years overshadowed the South speak eloquently of a national gain that is a loss. One hundred years ago the North freed its slaves. Later, when the constitution was adopted, many statesmen believed that slavery was losing its hold in the South. Jefferson said: "When I think that God is just I tremble for my country." In that hour the statesman prophesied that slavery would soon melt away like the vanishing snow of April. But when Whitney invented his gin and the raising of cotton became very lucrative slavery took on new life. It was Lord Brougham who first said that when slavery brought in 100 percent, while it was seen to be immoral, not all the navies of the world could stop it. Later, when it brought in 300 percent, it became a peculiar institution, patterned after the system of the patriarchs. But when it brought in 300 percent master and slave became a Christian relation, and slavery was baptized with quotations from the Old Testament.

But avarice could not forever blind men's eyes to scenes of sorrow, nor stop their ears to sounds of woe. When the horrors of the slave-market and the infamies of the cotton-field filled all the land with shame reformers arose, declaring that the attempt to compress and confine liberty would end in explosion. In that hour Northern men made tentative overtures looking to the purchase of all slaves. But slavery, Delilah-like, made the southern leaders drunk with the cup of sorcery. They scorned the proposition. In the light of subsequent events we see that in saving her institution the South lost it, and with it her wealth, while in losing her slaves the North gained her wealth. Under free labor the North doubled its population, its manufactories, its riches and waxed mighty. Under slave-labor the South dwindled in wealth and became only the empty shell of a state. The spark fired at Fort Sumter kindled a conflagration that swept through the sunny South like a devastating fire and revealed its inner poverty. When four years had passed by the farmhouses and factories were ruins, the village was a heap, the town a desolation. Graveyards were as populous as cities, each village had its company of cripples, the cry of the orphan and the widow filled all the land.

When Charles Darwin returned from his voyage around the world, he sent a generous contribution to the London Missionary Society. The great scientist had discovered that in lessening her wealth through missions England had saved her treasure through commerce. Traveling in foreign lands, Darwin noticed that the Christian teachers in schools that now touch 3,000,000 of young men and women in India, were really commercial agents for England's trade. In awakening the minds of the darkened millions the teacher had created a demand for books, news-papers and printing-presses. In awakening the sense of self-respect the teacher had created a demand for English clothing and the product of English looms. Also the influence of each home, with its comforts and conveniences, created a demand for English tools and improvements of labor. Summing up his observation, Lord Havelock said that each thousand dollars England had spent upon her missions had brought a return of a hundred thousand dollars through her commerce. Hitherto the interior of China has been closed to English merchants. To that dark land, therefore, England has sent 200 teachers whose homes are centers of light and in-spiration. When two-score years have passed English fleets will be taxed to the ut-most to carry to China, as now to India, her fabrics of cotton and wool, her presses, looms, sewing-machines, her pictures, her libraries. In giving of her wealth to found these destitute schools England will save it a hundred-fold and find new markets among 300,000,000 people.

Sacrifice is also the secret of influence. Long ago Cicero noted that tales of he-roes and eloquence and self-sacrifice cast a charm and spell upon the people. When men sacrifice ease, wealth, rank, life itself, the delight of the beholders knows no bounds. If we call the roll of the sons of greatness and influence we shall see that they are also the sons of self-sacrifice. The Grecian hero who lost his life that he might save his influence is typical of all the great leaders. Phocion was a patriot and martyr whose single error in judgment brought down a catastrophe upon his beloved Athens. When the fierce mob surrounded his house and prepared to beat down his doors, friends offered Phocion escape and shelter, but the hero went calmly forth to meet his death. When the day of execution arrived the cup of poison was handed to the other leaders first. The jailer was careful to see to it that before he reached Phocion he had only a few drops of hemlock left in his cup, but the hero drew out his purse and bade a youth run swiftly to buy more poison, saying to the onlookers: "Athens makes her patriots pay, even for dying." Losing his life, Phocion, found immortal influence.

The history of Holland's greatness is the history of one who saved liberty by losing his own life. William the Silent was a prince in station and in wealth, yet for Holland's sake made himself a beggar and an outlaw. He feared God, indeed, but not the batteries of Alva and Philip. His career reads like one who with naked fists captured a blazing cannon. Falling at last by the dagger of a hired assassin, he exclaimed: "I commit my poor people to God and myself to God's great captain, Christ." When he died little children cried in the streets. He lost his life, said his biographer, but saved his fame. And what shall we more say of Italy's hero, who wore his fiery fagots like a crown of gold; of Germany's hero, who lost his priestly rites, but gained the hearts of all mankind; of England's hero, whose very ashes were cast by enemies upon the River Severn, as if to float his influence out o'er all the world, of India's hero, William Carey, the English shoemaker, who founded for India an educational system now reaching millions of children and youth, who gave India literature, made five grammars and six dictionaries, and so used his commercial genius through his indigo plantation and factories that it made for him a million dollars in the interests of Christian missions? Of this great company, what can we say save that they won renown through self-renunciation! What they did makes weak and unworthy what we say. Just here let us remember that the statue of Jupiter was a figure so colossal that worshipers, unable to reach the divine forehead, cast their garlands at the hero's feet. For this law of sacrifice is the secret of the Messiah. Earth's great ones were taught it by their Master. Jesus Christ, "being rich, for our sakes became poor." Because the law of sacrifice is the law of the Savior, man gains life through death and renown through self-renunciation.

## THE GENTLENESS OF TRUE GIANTHOOD.

"A gentleman's first characteristic is that fineness of structure in the body which renders it capable of the most delicate sensation; and of structure in the mind which renders it capable of the most delicate sympathies--one may say, simply 'fineness of nature.' This is, of course, compatible with heroic bodily strength and mental firmness, in fact, heroic strength is not conceivable without such delicacy. Elephantine strength may drive its way through a forest and feel no touch of the boughs, but the white skin of Homer's Atrides would have felt a bent rose leaf, yet subdue its feeling in glow of battle, and behave itself like iron. I do not mean to call an elephant a vulgar animal, but if you think about him carefully you will find that his non-vulgarity consists in such gentleness as is possible to elephantine nature, not in his insensitive hide, nor in his clumsy foot, but in the way he will lift his foot if a child lies in his way and in his sensitive trunk, and still more sensitive mind, and capability of pique on points of honor. Hence it will follow that one of the probable signs of high-breeding in men generally will be their kindness and mercifulness."--***Modern Painters***.

History has never known another such an enthusiasm for a hero as the multitude once felt toward Jesus Christ. There have indeed been times when such patriots as Garibaldi, Kossuth and Lincoln have kindled in men an enthusiasm akin to adoration and worship. Yet let us hasten to confess that the qualities calculated to quicken men into raptures of devotion appeared in these patriots only in fragmentary form, while they dwelt in Christ in full-orbed majesty and splendor. The welcome Chicago gave to Grant upon his return from his journey around the world; the enthusiasm excited by Kossuth when in 1851 he drove through Broadway, New York; the wave of gratitude that swept over the Italian multitude when Garibaldi appeared in Florence--all these are events that bear witness to society's devotion to its patriots and heroes. But, be it remembered, these scenes occurred but once in the history of each of these great men.

It stirs wonder in us, therefore, that Christ's every journey across the fields took on the aspect of a triumphal procession, while His popularity waxed with familiarity and the increasing years. Indeed, full oft the rapture men felt toward Him amounted to an intoxication and an ecstasy of devotion. True it is that men now look upon Him through a blaze of light, and, remembering His achievements for art, liberty and learning, have stained His name through and through with lustrous colors. As at eventide we look out upon the sun through white and golden clouds that the sun itself has lifted, so do we behold the carpenter's son standing forth under the dazzling light of nearly two thousand years of history, while the heart colors His name with all that is noblest in human aspiration and achievement.

Nevertheless, be it instantly confessed that from the very beginning this divine Teacher exhibited qualities that kindled in men an enthusiasm that amounted to transcendent delight. The time was when scholars attempted to explain His influence over the multitude by portraying Him with a halo of light about His head. Fortunately these ideas that robbed men of all fellowship with their divine brother have perished, and now we know that there was nothing unusual about His appearance, nor did any effulgent light blaze forth from His person. Whether or not unique beauty of face and form was His we do not know. Coins and statues portray for us the Roman emperors and the Greek scholars. Yet art has broken down utterly in the attempt to combine in one face Christ's majesty and meekness, strength and gentleness, suffering and victory. All that we can know of His personal appearance must be gained through imagination, as it clothed Him with those traits that alone cannot account for His influence over the multitudes. What sweet allurement in the face that made children leap into His arms! What winsome benignity that made mothers feel that His touch would return the babe with double worth into the parent's bosom!

Purity in others has been cold and chaste as ice. How strange that in Him purity had an irresistible fascination, so that the corruptest and wickedest felt drawn unto Him, and "depravity itself bowed down and wept in the presence of divinity." What all-forgiving love, what all-cleansing love, in one who by a mere look could dissolve in repentant tears men long hardened by vice and crime! What an atmosphere of power He must have carried, that by one beam from His eye He could smite to the very ground the soldiers who confronted Him!

Did ever man have such a genius for noble friendship? What bosom words He used! What love pressure in all His speech! How were His words laden with double meanings, so that hearing one thing, men also heard another, even as they who hear the sound of the distant sea, knowing that the sound they hear is but a breath of the great infinite ocean that heaves beyond in the dim, vast dark. Among all the heroes of time He walks solitary by the greatness of His power, His beauty and the wonder of love His personality excited. Standing in the presence of some glorious cathedral or gallery, beholding the Parthenon or pyramids, the rugged mountain or the beautiful landscape, emotion and imagination are sometimes so deeply stirred that men lose command of themselves and break into transports of admiration. But the enthusiasm evoked by mountain or statue or canvas is as nothing compared to the rapturous devotion felt by the multitude for this One, who united in full splendor all those eminent qualities of mind and heart that all the ages and generations have in vain sought to emulate. High over all the other worthies He rises like a star riding in untroubled splendor above the low-browed hills.

In all ages great men have educated themselves by reading the biography of ancient worthies, and emulating the example of the heroes of antiquity. Great has been the influence of these reformers and philosophers, statesmen and poets, hanging in the heavens above men and raining down inspiration upon the human imagination. Yet from all the worthies of the past, and all modern heroes, man has drawn less of inspiration and personal influence than from the single example of this ideal Christ. Passing by His influence upon institutions, education, art and literature, we shall do well to consider how His example has instructed man in the art of a right carriage of the faculties in the home and market-place. In the last analysis, Jesus Christ is the only perfect gentleman our earth has ever known--in comparison with whom all the Chesterfields seem boors. For nothing taxes a man so heavily as the task of maintaining smooth, pleasant and charitable relations with one's fellows. And Christ alone was able always to meet storm with calm, hate with love, scowls with smiles, plottings with confidence, envy and bitterness with unruffled tranquility.

In all His relations with His friends and enemies the quality that crowns His method of living and challenges our thought is the gentleness of His bearing. Matchless the mingled strength and beauty of His life, yet gentleness was the flower and fruitage of it all. For in Him the lion and the lamb dwelt together. Oak and rock were there, and also vine and flower. Weakness is always rough. Only giants can be gentle. Tenderness is an inflection of strength. No error can be greater than to suppose that gentleness is mere absence of vigor. Weakness totters and tugs at its burden. When the dwarf that attended Ivanhoe at the tournament lifted the bleeding sufferer he staggered under his heavy burden. Weakness made him stumble and caused the wounded knight intense pain. When the giant of the brawny arm and the unconquered heart came, he lifted the unconscious sufferer like a feather's weight and without a jar bore him away to a secure hiding-place for healing and recovering. He who studies the great men of yesterday will find in the last analysis that gentleness has always been the test of gianthood, and fine considerateness the measure of manhood and the gauge of personal worth. No other hero moving through the crowds has ever been so courteously gentle, so sweetly considerate in his personal bearing as this Christ--who never failed to kindle in men transports of delight and enthusiasm.

The crying fault of our generation is its lack of gentleness. Our age is harsh when it judges, brutal when it blames and savage in its severity. Carlyle, emptying vials of scorn upon the people of England, numbering his generation by "thirty millions, mostly fools," is typical of the publicists, authors and critics who pelt their brother man with contemptuous scorn. The author of "Robert Elsmere" exhibits that polished scholar and brilliant student as one who gave up teaching because he could find no audience on a level with his ability or worthy of his instruction. Having begun by despising others, he ends by despising himself. Now the popularity of Elsmere's character witnesses to the fact that our generation includes a large number of cynics who scorn their fellows and in Elsmere see themselves as "in an open glass." To-day this tendency toward harshness of judgment has become more pronounced, and there seems to be no leader so noble as to escape brutal criticism and no movement whose white flag may not be smirched by mud-slingers. What epithets are hurled at each new idea! What torrents of ridicule are emptied out upon each social movement!

The fact that society has oftentimes destroyed its noblest geniuses avails little for the restraint of harshness. For years England was wildly merry at Turner's expense. The newspapers cartooned his paintings. Reviews spoke of them as "color blotches." The rich over their champagne made merry at the great artist's expense. After a while men found a little respite from the mad chase for wealth and pleasure and discovered that Turner's extreme examples represented peculiar moods in nature, seen only by those who had traveled as widely as had Turner, while his great landscapes were as rich in imaginative quality as those of any artist of all ages. Only when it was too late, only when harshness had broken the man's heart, and scorn had fatally wounded his genius, did scholars begin to adorn their pages by references to Turner's fame, did the rich begin to pay fabulous sums for the very pictures they had once despised, the nation set apart the best room in its gallery for Turner's works, while the people wove for his white tombstone wreaths they had denied his brow and paid his dead ashes honors refused his living spirit.

In similar vein we remember the English-speaking world has recently been celebrating the anniversary of the birth of Keats, who is the only pure Greek in all English literature, for whose imagination "a thing of beauty was a joy forever," and whose genius in divining the secrets of the beautiful amounted to inspiration. We know now that no poet in all time, who died so young, has left so much that is precious. Scholars are not wanting who believe that had he lived to see his maturity Keats would have ranked with the five great poets of the first order of genius. Yet the publication of his volume of verse received from "Blackwood" and the "Quarterly" only contempt and bitter scorn. Waxing bold, the penny-a-liners grew savage, until the very skies rained lies and bitter slanders upon poor Keats. Sensitive, soon he was wounded to death. After a week of sleeplessness, he arose one morning to find a bright red spot upon his handkerchief. "That is arterial blood," said he; "that drop is my death-warrant; I shall die." And so, when he was one-and-twenty, friends lifted above the boy's dust a marble slab, upon which was written: "Here lies one whose name was writ in water." Now his name shines like a star, while low down and bespattered with mud are the names of those whose cruel criticisms helped to kill the boy and whose only claim to immortality is their brutality.

Witness also the contempt our age once visited upon Browning, whose mind is slowly becoming recognized as one of the rich-gold minds of our century. Witness the sport over Ruskin's "Munera Pulveris," and the scornful reception given Carlyle's "Sartor Resartus." Now that a few years have passed, those who once reviled are teaching their children the pathway to the graves of the great. The harshness of the world's treatment of its greatest teachers makes one of the most pathetic chapters in history. God gives each nation only a few men of supreme talent. Gives it, for greatness is not made; it is found as is the gold. Gold cannot be made out of mud; it is uncovered. And God gives each generation a few men of the first order; and when they have created truth and beauty they have the right while they live to kindness and sympathy, not harshness and cynicism. No youth winning the first goal of his ambition was ever injured by knowing that his father's face did not flush with pride, while his mother's eyes were filled with happy tears, in joy of his first victory. No noble lover but girds himself for a second struggle the more resolutely for knowing that his noble mistress rejoiced in his first conquest. Frost itself is not more destructive to harvest fields than harshness is to the creative faculties. Strange that Florence gave Dante exile in exchange for his immortal poem! Strange that London gave Milton threats of imprisonment for the manuscript of "Paradise Lost!" Passing strange that until his career was nearly run universities visited upon John Ruskin only scorn and contumely, that ruined his health and broke his heart, withholding the wreath until, as he said pathetically, his only "pleasure was in memory, his ambition in heaven," and he knew not what to do with his laurel leaves save "lay them wistfully upon his mother's grave." In every age the critics that have refused honor to its worthies, living, have heaped gifts high upon the graves of its dead.

That generation and individual must be far from perfect that is characterized by the presence of harshness and the absence of gentleness. With a great blare of trumpets our century has been praised for its ingenuity, its wealth and comforts, its instruments, refinement and culture. But history tells of no man who has carried his genius up to such supreme excellence that society has forgotten his vice or forgiven the faults that marred his rare gifts. What genius had De Quincey! Marvelous the myriad-minded Coleridge! The opium-habit, however, was a vice that eclipsed their fame and robbed them of half their rightful influence. Voltaire's style was so faultlessly perfect that if the sentences lying across his page had been strings of pearls they could have been no more beautiful. But Voltaire's excesses make a black mark across the white page before each reader's mind. Rousseau's writings are so melodious that, long after laying aside the book the ear would be filled with the sound of delicious music were it not that the reader seems ever to hear the moan of the four children whose unnatural father, without even giving them a name, placed them in the foundling-asylum.

Early Carlyle wooed and won one of the most brilliant girls of his day, whose signal talent shone in the crowded drawing-rooms of London like a sapphire blazing among pebbles. Yet her husband lacked gentleness. Slowly harshness crept into Carlyle's voice. Soon the wife gave up her favorite authors to read the husband's notes; then she gave up all reading to relieve him of details; at last her very being was placed on the altar of sacrifice--fuel to feed the flame of his fame and genius. Long before the end came she was submerged and almost forgotten. One day two distinguished foreign authors called upon Mr. and Mrs. Carlyle. For an hour the philosopher poured forth vehement tirade against the commercial spirit, while the good wife never once opened her lips. At last the author ceased talking, and there was silence for a time. Suddenly Carlyle thundered: "Jane, stop breathing so loud!" Long years before Jane had stopped doing everything else except breathe. And so, obedient to the injunction, a few days afterward she ceased "breathing so loud."

When a few weeks had gone by Carlyle discovered, through reading her journal, that his wife had for want of affection frozen and starved to death within his home like some poor traveler who had fallen in the snows beyond the door. For years, without his realizing it, she had kept all the wheels oiled, kept his body in health and his mind in happiness. Only when it was too late did the husband realize that his fame was largely his wife's. Then did the old man begin his pathetic pilgrimage to his wife's grave, where Froude often found him murmuring: "If I had only known! If I had only known!" For all his supreme gifts and rare talents were marred by harshness. Intellectual brilliancy weighs light as punk against the gold of gentleness and character. Half Carlyle's books, weighted by a gentle, noble spirit, would have availed more for social progress than these many volumes with the bad taste they leave in the mouth. The sign of ripeness in an apple, a peach, is beauty, and the test of character is gentleness and kindness of heart.

One of the crying needs of society is a revival of gentleness and of a refined considerateness in judging others. There is no disposition that cuts at the very root of character like harshness, and there is nothing that blights happiness and breeds discord like unlovingness and severity of judgment. We hear much of industrial strife, social warfare and want of sympathy between the classes. Be it remembered, gentleness alone can be invoked to heal the breach. There is a legend that when Jacob with his family and flocks met Esau with his children and herds, the angels of God hovered in the air above the two brothers and began to rain gifts down upon their companies. Strangely enough, each forgetting the gifts falling in his own camp, rushed forth to pick up the gifts falling in that of his brother. There was anger stirred. Epithets and stones began to fly, until all the air was filled with flying weapons. In such a scrimmage the messengers of peace had no place. Soon the sound of receding wings died out of the air, the gifts ceased to fall and all things faded into the light of common day. This legend interprets to us how harshness breeds strife and robs man of his gifts from God and his happiness through his brother man.

Several years ago an industrial war was waged in the coal districts of England that cost that nation untold treasure. It is said that the strife grew out of harsh words between the leaders of the opposing factions. It seemed that the industrious and worthy poor men overlooked the fact that there were industrious and worthy rich men and insisted on speaking only of the idle and spendthrift rich. Then followed his opponent who, as an industrious and worthy rich man, insisted on ignoring the industrious and worthy poor, but spoke only of the idle and thriftless poor, the paupers and parasites. Soon gentleness was forgotten and harshness remembered. Soon there came the trampled cornfields and the bloody streets.

Teachers also need to learn the lesson of Arnold of Rugby. One day the great instructor spake harshly to a dull boy, who an hour afterward came to him with tearful eyes, and in a half-sobbing voice exclaimed; "But why are you angry, sir? I am doing my best." Then Arnold learned that a lesson easy for one mind may be a torture for another. So he begged the boy's pardon, and recognized the principle of gentleness that afterward made him the greatest instructor of his time.

Not war, not pestilence, not famine itself, produces for each generation so much misery and unhappiness as is wrought in the aggregate through the accumulated harshness of each generation. Blessed are the happiness-makers! Blessed are they who with humble talents make themselves like the mignonette, creators of fragrance and peace! Thrice blessed are they who with lofty talents emulate the vines that climbing high never forget to blossom, and the higher they climb do ever shed sweet blooms upon those beneath! No single great deed is comparable for a moment to the multitude of little gentlenesses performed by those who scatter happiness on every side and strew all life with hope and good cheer.

Life holds no motive for stimulating gentleness in man like the thought of the gentleness of God. Unfortunately, it seems difficult for man to associate delicacy and gentleness with vastness and strength. It was the misfortune of Greek philosophers and is, indeed, that of nearly all the modern theologians, to suppose that a perfect being cannot suffer. Both schools of thought conceive of God as sitting upon a marble throne, eternally young, eternally beautiful, beholding with quiet indifference from afar how man, with infinite blunderings, sufferings and tears makes his way forward. Yet He who holds the sun in the hollow of his hand, who takes up the isles as a very little thing, who counts the nations but as the dust in the balance, is also the gentle One. Like the wide, deep ocean, that pulsates into every bay and creek and blesses the distant isles with its dew and rain, so God's heart throbs and pulsates unto the uttermost parts of the universe, having a parent's sympathy for His children who suffer.

Indeed, the seer ranges through all nature searching out images for interpreting His all-comprehending gentleness. "Even the bruised reed he will not break." Lifting itself high in the air, a mere lead pencil for size, weighted with a heavy top, a very little injury shatters a reed. Some rude beast, in wild pursuit of prey, plunges through the swamp, shatters the reed, leaves it lying upon the ground, all bruised and bleeding, and ready to die. Such is God's gentleness that, though man make himself as worthless as a bruised reed; though by his ignorance, frailty and sin he expel all the manhood from his heart and life, and make himself of no more value than one of the myriad reeds in the world's swamps, still doth God say: "My gentleness is such that I will direct upon this wounded life thoughts that shall recuperate and heal, until at last the bruised reed shall rise up in strength, and judgment shall issue in victory."

And as God's gentleness would go one step further, there is added the tender lesson of the smoking flax. Our glowing electric bulbs suffer no injury from blasts, and our lamps have like strength. The time was, when, wakened by the cry of the little sufferer, the ancient mother sprang up to strike the tinder and light the wick in the cup of oil. Only with difficulty was the tinder kindled. Then how precious the spark that one breath of air would put out! With what eagerness did the mother guard the smoking flax! And in setting forth the gentleness of God it is declared that, with eyes of love, He searches through each heart, and if He find so much as a spark of good in the outcast, the publican, the sinner, He will tend that spark and feed it toward the love that shall glow and sparkle forever and ever; for evil is to be conquered, and God will not so much punish as exterminate sin from His universe. His strength is inflicted toward gentleness, His justice tempered with mercy, and all his attributes held in solution of love. No longer should medievalism becloud God's gentle face. Cleanse your thoughts, as once the artist in Milan cleansed the grime and soot from the wall where Dante's lustrous face was hidden.

With shouts and transports of joy and admiration men welcome the patriot or hero who in times of danger held the destiny of the people in his hands and never once betrayed it. And let each intellect soar without hindrance, and the heart pour itself out before God in a freshet of divine love. Great is the genius of Plato or Bacon, revealing itself in tides of thought, but greater and richer is the genius of the heart that is conscious of vast, deep fountains of love, that may be poured forth in generous tides before the God whose throne is mercy, whose face is light, whose name is love, whose strength is gentleness, whose considerateness is our pledge of pardon, peace and immortality.

# THE THUNDER OF SILENT FIDELITY:
# A STUDY OF THE INFLUENCE OF LITTLE THINGS.

"We treat God with irreverence by banishing Him from our thoughts, not by referring to His will on slight occasions. His is not the finite authority or intelligence which cannot be troubled with small things. There is nothing so small but that we may honor God by asking His guidance of it, or insult Him by taking it into our own hands; and what is true of Deity is equally true of His Revelation. We use it most reverently when most habitually; our insolence is in ever acting without reference to it, our true honoring of it is in its universal application. I have been blamed for the familiar introduction of its sacred words. I am grieved to have given pain by so doing, but my excuse must be my wish that those words were made the ground of every argument and the test of every action. We have them not often enough on our lips, nor deeply enough in our memories, nor loyally enough in our lives. The snow, the vapour and the strong wind fulfil His word. Are our acts and thoughts lighter and wilder than these, that we should forget it?"--*Ruskin*.

"I expect to pass through this life but once. If there is any kindness or any good thing I can do to my fellow-beings let me do it now. I shall pass this way but once."--- *William Penn*.

Schliemann, uncovering marbles upon which Phidias and his followers carved out immortality for themselves, has not wrought more effectually for the increase of knowledge than have those excavators in Egypt who have uncovered the Rosetta stone, with other manuscripts of brick and marble. Of all these instructive tablets and tombs, none are more interesting than one picturing forth a national festival in the Jewish capital. Upon his canvas of stone the unknown artist portrays for us Herod's temple with its outer courts and columns and its massive walls.

We see the public square crowded with merchants and traders, who have come in from the great cities of the world to this festival of the fathers. With solemn pageantry, these Jews, who were the bankers and merchants of that far-off age, march through the streets toward the gate that is called Beautiful. In the vast parade are men notable by their princely wealth in Ephesus and Antioch, in Alexandria and Rome. We see one advancing with his retinue of servants, another with the train which corresponds to his wealth. One group the artist exhibits as characteristic. Advancing before their lord and master are four servants, who lift up in the presence of admiring spectators a platter upon which lies a heap of shining gold. The murmur of admiration that runs through the crowd is sweeter to the old merchant's ear than any music of harp or human voice. Passing by the treasury, what gifts are cast upon the resounding table! How heavy the bars of gold! What silver plate! What pearls and jewels! How rich the fabrics and hangings for the temple! As at St. Peter in the sixteenth century, so in Christ's day it seemed as if the whole world were being swept for treasures for enriching this glorious temple.

But when the lions of the procession had all passed by, there followed also the crowd of stragglers. From this post of observation we are told that Christ saw a poor widow advancing. With falling tears, yet with exquisite grace and tenderness, she cast in two mites, or one half-penny, then passed on to worship him whom she loved, all unconscious of the fact that she had also passed into immortality. For the noise of the gold falling into the resounding chest has long since died away. Jerusalem itself is in ruins. The old temple with its magnificence has gone to decay. The proud thrones and monarchies have all fallen into dust. But the silent fidelity of this obscure woman is a voice that thunders down the long aisles of time. A thousand times hath she encouraged heroism in poet and parent. Ten thousand times hath she been an inspiration to reformers and martyrs! Love and fidelity have embalmed her deed and lent her immortality. In the very center of the world's civilization stands her monument. For her Arc de Triomphe has been built in the human heart. Her monument does not appeal to the eye; it is not carved in stone; yet it is more permanent than gold, and her fame outshines all flashing jewels. While love and admiration endure the story of her humble fidelity shall abide indestructible!

The great Italian first noted that thrice only did Christ stretch forth his hand to build a monument, and each time it was to immortalize a deed of humble fidelity. Once a disciple gave a cup of cold water to one of God's little ones, and won thereby imperishable renown. Once a woman broke an alabaster box for her master, and, lo! her deed has been like a broken vase, whose perfume has exhaled for two thousand years, and shall go on diffusing sweetness to the end of time. Last of all, after the rich men of Alexandria had cast their rattling gold into the brazen treasury, a poor widow cast a speck of dust called two mites, and, lo! this humble deed gave her enduring recollection.

It seems that immortal renown is achieved not so much by the solitary deed of greatness as by humble fidelity to life's details, and that modest Christian living that regards small deeds and minor duties. Ours is a world in which life's most perfect gifts and sweetest blessings are little things. Take away love, daily work, sweet sleep, and palaces become prisons and gold seems contemptible. The classic poet tells of Kind [Transcriber's note: King?] Midas, to whom was offered whatsoever he wished, and whose avarice led him to choose the golden touch. But lo! his blessing became a curse. Rising to dress he found himself shivering in a coat with threads of gold. Going into his garden he stooped to breathe the perfume of the roses, and, lo! the dewy petals became yellow points that pierced his face. Breakfasting, the bread became metal in his mouth. Lifting a goblet the water became a solid mass. Swinging his little daughter in his arms one kiss turned the sweet child into a cold statue. A single hour availed to drive happiness from Midas' heart. In an agony of despair he besought the gods for simple things. He asked for one cup of cold water, one cluster of fruit and his little daughter's loving heart and hand.

And as with wealth, so wisdom without life's little things is impotent for happiness. Genius hath its charm; nevertheless, the wisest of men have also been the saddest of men. The story of literary greatness is a piteous tale. History tells of many beautiful and gifted girls who have married scholars for their genius, fame and position. When these honors were theirs they wakened to discover that all were less than nothing, since tenderness refused its mite and sympathy gave cot its cup of cold water. Home and fame became dungeons in which the soul sat and famished for love's little courtesies.

For no palace was ever so beautiful, no royal wine quaffed from vessels of gold was ever so sweet as to satisfy hearts famishing for one mite of that heavenly manna love prepares, or one cup filled with kindness.

Down in a corner of a window of an English palace may be found faint lines scratched with a woman's diamond. What a tragedy in those words, "My prison!" It seems the sweet girl, Jane Grey, entered her palace with a leaping heart, but her lord had no time to break upon her white forehead the tiny box of life's ointment. Hers was the palace; hers also a thousand rich gifts called titles, lands, castles, maids of honor, dresses, jewels. Yet because the castles held no sweet courtesies the journal of that beautiful girl reminds us of some young bird that beats with bloody wings against the bars of an iron cage. For life is made up not of joys few and intense, but of joys many and gentle. Great happiness is the sum of many small drops. God makes the days that are channels of mighty and tumultuous joys to be few and far between. For highly spiced joys exhaust. All who seek intense pleasure will find not enjoyment but yearnings for enjoyment. Happiness is in simple things; a cup of cold water, health and a perfect day; dreamless sleep, honest toil, the esteem of the worthy, the caresses of little children, a love that waxes with the increasing years.

Our appreciation of the principle that greatness of any form is an accumulation of little deeds will be freshened by an outlook upon nature's method. The old science unveiled the universe as a divine thought rushing into instant form, stars and suns being sparks struck out on the anvil of omnipotence. The new science has found that earth's every atom has been slowly polished by an infinite artisan and architect. If we descend into the sea we shall find that the reefs and islands against which the tides of the Pacific dash in vain are built of coral insects, whose every organ exhibits the delicate skill of a diamond or snowflake. If we stand upon the fruitful plain where men build cities we shall discern that each flake of the rich soil represents the perfect crystallization of drops of melted granite. If we take the wings of the morning and dwell upon the summit of the Matterhorn there also we find that the mountain hath its height and majesty through particles themselves weak and little. For the geologist who analyzes the topmost peak of the Alpine ridge must go back to a little flake of mica, that ages and ages ago floated along some one of earth's rivers, too light to sink, too feeble to find the fiber of a lichen, therefore dropped into the ooze of mire and decay. Yet hardened by earth's processes, the day came when that flake of mica was lifted up upon the mountain's peak, wrought into the strength of imperishable iron, "rustless by the air, infusible by the flame, capping the very summit of the Alpine tower. Above it--that little obscure mica flake--the north winds rage, yet all in vain, below it--the feeble mica flake--the snowy hills lie bowing themselves like flocks of sheep, and the distant kingdoms fade away in unregarded blue."[3] Around it--the weak, wave-drifted mica flake--booms all the artillery of storms, when electric arrows with blunted points fall back from its front, as it lifts its might and majesty toward the enduring stars.

If ages ago the sages said, God is not in the earthquake, nor in the storm, but in the still small voice, now science reaffirms the declaration that omnipotence is revealed not so much through awful cataclysms and earthquake forces as through the silent agents and hidden processes that make the plains to be fruitful and hillsides to be rich in corn. In the past astronomy has been the favorite science, emphasizing the distant stars and suns. The science of the future is to be chemistry, emphasizing atoms and elements. Journeying outward in pursuit of the footsteps of God, advancing upon his distant and dizzy march, man's vision faints and falls upon the horizon beyond which are indiscernible splendors. Journeying inward upon the wings of the microscope, we shall find that there is another realm of beauty beyond which the utmost vision of man cannot pierce. For before the microscope "the last discernible particle dies out of sight with the same perfect glory on it as on the last orb that glimmers in the skirts of the universe." If God is throned in the clouds He is also tabernacled in the dewdrop and palaced in the bud and blossom.

The history of nations and individuals teaches us that the greatest gifts are poor and empty and the most signal talents worthless if the small things be not done, the two mites be not given. For life is marred by little infelicities and ruined by little errors. The broken columns and marble heaps in lands where once were cities represent destructions not so much through tornadoes and earthquakes as through small vices and unnoticed sins. In modern life also, journeying through city and forest and field, the economist returns to tell us that life's chief wastes are through little enemies and foes. It is a minute bug that steals the golden berry from the wheat; it is a tiny germ upon the leaf that blights the budding peach and pear, it is a

3   Ruskin's Modern Painters, Vol. iv., page 284.
   [Transcriber's note: In the original book, there was no footnote symbol in the page where this footnote appeared. I've made a best guess of its intended location.]

rough spot upon the potato that fills all Ireland with fear of famine; it is a worm that bores through the planks of the ship's hull and alarms old seacaptains as approaching battleships could not.

The enemies of human life are not enemies that fill man's streets with banners and charging cannon. We wage war against the dust mote ambushed in the sunbeam; we fight against weapons hurled from those battleships called drops of impure water; we wrestle with those hosts whose broadsides invisible rise from streets foul, or fall from poisoned clouds. Such enemies that lurk in dampness and darkness, a thousand fall at thy side and ten thousand at thy right hand. That great catastrophe that overtook Holland a century ago is not explained by a tidal wave that pierced through the dikes; the disaster was through the crawfishes that opened tiny holes and, weakening the bulwarks, let in the onrushing sea.

It was but a trifling error also that robbed the generations of one of man's divinest pictures. Three hundred years ago the monks made tight and strong the roof above the room where was Da Vinci's "Last Supper." A thousand tiles were fastened down and all save one were perfect. The one hid a secret hole. When months had passed and the driving storm came from the right direction the rain found out that hidden fault and, rushing in, a flood of drops streamed down o'er the wall and made a great black mark across the noble painting, and ruined the central face forever.

Human life is ruined through the absence of humble virtues and the presence of little faults. There is no man so great, no gift so brilliant, but let it be whispered that there is falseness in the life of the hero, and immediately his greatness is dwarfed, his eloquence becomes a trick, his authority is impaired. Reading Robert Burns' poems, he seems wiser than all the scholars, wittier than all the humorists, more courtly than princes. His genius blazes like a torch among the tapers. But watching this son of genius and of liberty weave a net for his own feet, and fashion a snare for his own faculties, with wistful hearts we long, as one has said, "to hear the exulting and triumphant cry of the strong man coming to himself, I will arise." But he loved the barroom more than the library, and so fell on death at seven and thirty, and lost his right to rule as a king o'er men's hearts and lives. Byron, too, and Goethe had gifts so resplendent that in kings' palaces they shine like diamonds amid the pebbles. What a constellation of gifts was theirs! Culture, sanity, imagination, wit, courage, vigor--all these stars were grouped in their mental constellations! Yet little vices dethroned these kings and made them plebeian. It is the absence of little virtues and sweet domestic graces that seem trifling as the two mites that robs the Roman poets and orators of their power over us. They had urbanites indeed, flowers, music, art, oratory, letters, song. The events of each day were executed like a piece of music, and even their sarcophagi were covered with scenes of feasting and revelry. But they were not true; and that false note jars through all their pages. Harshness in the poet and pride in the orator make their refinement and culture seem but skin deep.

We note that Pompeii was a paradise built beside a crater. The traveler tells us if we strike the rocky earth it rings hollow. Close by the calm lake is a boiling spring. In the very heart of the orange groves rises a column of smoke and steam. "The mist of lava jars on the music of summer, the scent of sulphur mingles with the scent of roses." Not for a moment can the traveler forget that beneath all this opulence of color and fragrance rages a colossal furnace. Thus the harshness and selfishness found in the eloquence and poetry of the ancient writers rob us of all joy in their splendid gifts. We yield homage only to the greatness that is also goodness. To ten-talent power the hero must also add tenderness to his own, kindness to the weak, unfailing sympathy to all. No giant is a full giant until he is also gentle, stooping to give his two mites to the weak, bearing to the weary his cup of cold water, ever emulating that hero, Sir Philip Sydney, wounded sorely indeed, but pushing away the canteen because the soldier, suffering great pain, had greater need.

In one of his essays Lowell notes that the great reform monuments are the humble deeds of humble persons, taken up and repeated by an entire people. The final victories for liberty and religion are emblazoned upon monuments and celebrated in song and story, but the beginnings of these achievements for mankind are often given over to obscurity and forgetfulness. Our age makes much of the "Red Cross" movement. Hardly fifty years have passed since two English girls boarded the steamer that was to carry them to the Crimea. Upon the distant battlefields, with their deserted cannon, wounded horses and dying men, at first these gentle girls seemed strangely out of place. The hospitals were full; neglected soldiers were lying in the thickets, whither they had crawled to die. Counseling with none, these brave girls moved across the battlefields like angels of mercy. Many years have passed. Now these nurses bring hope to every battlefield, and minister to every stricken Armenia, for the story of that sweet girl has filled the earth with "King's Daughters." One hundred years ago also England left her orphan babes to grow up in the country poorhouse, midst surroundings often vulgar, profane and brutal. One day two sweet babes, unnamed and unwelcomed, lay in the garret of a county-house in the outskirts of London. Then a poor, half-witted spinster, hearing of the young mother's death, found her way to the garret, brooded o'er the babes with all the dignity of our Mother of Sorrows, took the babes to her heart and planned how, with six shillings a week, she might keep bread in three hungry mouths. Four years passed by, and one day the lord of the manor stayed a moment before this woman's hovel and heard her prayer for the two boys clinging to her skirts. Soon the story of the woman's mercy was heard in every English pulpit, and in every town men and women made their way to the county-houses to take away the orphan babes and found instead some asylum for God's little ones. Now noble men in distant lands plan homes and shelter for little children, and the work of the obscure woman is a part of the history of reform.

Humble also is the origin of the anti-slavery movement that won its final victory at Appomattox. A century and more ago a young Moravian made his way to Jamaica as a Herald of Christ and his message of good-will. The horrors of slavery in that far-off time cannot be understood by our age. Then each week some African slaver landed with its cargo of naked creatures. Slaves were so cheap that it was simpler to kill them with rapid work and purchase new ones than to care for the wants of captives weakened by several summers. What horrors under overseers in the field! What outrages in slave-market and pen! So grievous were the wrongs negroes suffered at white men's hands that they would not listen to this young teacher. At last, despairing of their confidence, the brave youth had himself sold as a slave and wrought in the fields under the overseer's lash. Fellowship with their sufferings won their confidence and love. When the day's task was done the poor creatures crowded about him to receive Christ's cup of cold water. Long years after the young hero had fallen upon the sugar plantation his story came to the ears of young Wilberforce and armed him with courage invincible against England's traffic in flesh and blood. Soon Parliament freed the West India slaves and Lincoln emancipated our freedmen. But side by side with the heroes of liberty famed through monument and solemn oration, let us mention the young Moravian hero who loved

Christ's little ones, and in giving "two mites and a cup of cold water," lost his life, indeed, but found immortal fame.

This modest deed that bought renown also tells us that enduring remembrance is possible for all. Great deeds the majority cannot do. Two-talent men march in millions, but the ten-talent men are few and far between. Many scientists--one Newton. Thousands of poets--but the Elizabethan eras are separated by centuries. Great is the company of the orators--but to each generation only one Webster and one Clay. As each continent hath but one mountain range, so the elect minds stand isolated in the ages. All greatness is mysterious, and like God's throne, genius is girt about with clouds and darkness. If great men are infrequent, the world's need of great men is as occasional. Society advances in happiness and culture, not through striking, dramatic acts, but through myriads of unnumbered and unnoticed deeds.

Even the heroes dying upon the battlefield ask not for Plato nor Bacon, but for a cup of cold water. To Benedict Arnold, dying in his garret, came a physician, who said, "Is there anything you wish?" and heard this answer; "Only a friend." Traitors sometimes each of us also. Traitors to our deepest convictions and our highest ideals, and in the hours when the fever of discontent burns fiercely within us, and the mind seems half-delirious in its trouble, we also ask for a friend bringing a mite of sympathy and a cup of cold water. Let us confess it--we are all famishing for love and the kind word that says: "In your Gethsemane you are not alone."

God secures for us our happiness, not through speech about the heavens and firmament, but through the comfort that comes through speech over little things. He feeds the birds, adorns the lily, clothes the grass, numbers man's troubles. He is the Shepherd seeking the one sheep, the father waiting for the lost son. His kingdom is a little leaven working in the world's meal, His truth being no larger than a grain of mustard-seed. Above each little one bows some guardian angel beholding the face of its heavenly Father. And He who unites grains of sand for making planets and rays of light for glorious suns, and blades of grass for the solid splendor of field and pasture and drops of water for the ocean that blesses every continent with its dew and rain, teaches us also that great principles will organize the little words, little prayers, little aspirations and little services into the full-orbed splendor of an enduring character and an immortal fame.

Happily none need journey far nor search long for opportunities of humble fidelity. Into our midst come each year thousands of boys who are strangers in the great city. Passing along the streets these lonely lads behold each horse having some friendly hand to care for it. Yea! each sleek dog hath some owner's name engraven on the collar for the neck. But for the youth, weeks pass by, and no face lifts a friendly smile, no hand is outstretched in gentle kindness, and oft the thought is bitter: "No man careth for my soul." The youth who sits in the seat beside you asks only that the leaflet be shared in brotherliness, and you may lift upon the discouraged one a smile that saith; "Once the battle went sore with me, also, but be of good cheer, you shall overcome." Such friendliness is the two mites that buy enduring rembrance. For if each must fight his own battles, face for himself the spectres of doubt, and slay them; if each must be his own surgeon and draw the iron from the soul, still sympathy is a precious boon, and it is given to man to give the cup of tenderness to the warrior sorely wounded in life's battle. In ancient times when men's cabins were built on the edge of the wilderness, not yet cleared of wild beasts, sometimes the little ones wandered from the path and were lost in the forest, until the cry of terror revealed the awful danger that threatened and caused the mother to speed forth with winged feet and lift her body as a shield against the enemy. Daily these scenes are re-enacted, not in songs and dramas, but through the work of those who rescue the city's children from squalor, filth and sin. What redemptions' man's little deeds do bring!

For $30,000 Peter Faneuil bought immortality and forever associated his name with liberty. To-day that amount will erect the social settlement in the needy quarter of some city and give hundreds of young people opportunity and field for Bible-schools, kindergartens, nursery, gymnasium, mothers' classes, men's clubs, singing-schools and also associate man's name with the happiness and civilization of an entire community. Mammon will care for the children of strength and good fortune, and fame will guard the sons of success; let us guard the weak and lowly. In the Roman triumph, when a general came home with his spoils, many captives went with his chariot up to the capital. And happy 'twill be for us if in the hour when the sunset gun shall sound and we pass beyond the flood God's little ones mourn us with tears of gratitude while all the trumpets sound for us on the other side.

# INFLUENCE, AND THE STRATEGIC ELEMENT IN OPPORTUNITY.

"And now, gentlemen, was this vast campaign fought without a general? If Trafalgar could not be won without the mind of a Nelson, or Waterloo without the mind of a Wellington, was there no one mind to lead these innumerable armies, on whose success depended the future of the whole human race? Did no one marshal them in that impregnable convex front, from the Euxine to the North Sea? No one guide them to the two great strategic centres of the Black Forest and Trieste? No one cause them, blind barbarians without maps or science, to follow those rules of war without which victory in a protracted struggle is impossible: and by the pressure of the Huns behind, force on their flagging myriads to an enterprise which their simplicity fancied at first beyond the powers of mortal men? Believe it who will; I cannot.

"But while I believe that not a stone or a handful of mud gravitates into its place without the will of God; that it was ordained, ages since, into what particular spot each grain of gold should be washed down from an Australian quartz reef, that a certain man might find it at a certain moment and crisis of his life--if I be superstitious enough (as thank God I am) to hold that Creed, shall I not believe that though this great war had no general upon earth, it may have had a general in Heaven; and that in spite of all their sins the hosts of our forefathers were the hosts of God?"--***Charles Kingsley***.

The history of a Jewish battle includes a dramatic incident. In the thick of the fight an officer brought to one of his soldiers an important prisoner. "Keep thou this man," said he, "with the utmost vigilance. Upon his person hang the issues of this campaign. His skill in leading the enemy, his courage and treachery have cost our side many lives. If by any means thou shalt suffer him to escape thy life shall be for his life."

Then, straining more tightly the cords knotted around the prisoner's hands and feet, the officer turned and plunged again into the thick of the fight. From that moment the soldier's one duty was to guard the prisoner whose escape would work such havoc.

Strangely enough, he became negligent. Careless, he leaned his bow and spear against the tent. Hungry, he busied himself with baking a few small cakes. Weary, he cast himself upon the ground, dozing upon his elbow. Suddenly a noise startled his nap. He sprang up just in time to see his prisoner make one leap, then disappear into the thicket.

A concealed knife had cut the thongs. Negligence had let "slip the dogs of war." That night when the general returned to his tent he found the prisoner had escaped.

Fronting his master the terror-stricken soldier had no excuse to offer save this; "While thy servant was busy here and there the man was gone." Gone opportunity!--and lightning could not equal its swift flight. Gone forever opportunity!--and the wings of seraphim could not overtake and bring it back. Gone honor, gone fidelity, gone good name!--all lost irretrievably. For though dying be long delayed, coming at last death would find the soldier's task unfulfilled. From "It might have been," and "It is too late," God save us all! For not Infinity himself can reverse the wheel of events and bring back lost opportunities.

The genius of opportunity lies in its strategic element. In every opportunity two or more forces meet in such a way that the one force so lends itself to the other as momentarily to yield plasticity. Nature is full of these strategic times. Iron passes into the furnace cold and unyielding; coming out it quickly cools and refuses the mold; but midway is a moment when fire so lends itself to iron, and iron so yields its force to flame as that the metal flows like water.

This brief plastic moment is the inventor's opportunity, when the metal will take on any shape for use or beauty. Similarly the fields offer a strategic time to the husbandman. In February the soil refuses the plow, the sun refuses heat, the sky refuses rain, the seed refuses growth. In May comes an opportune time when all forces conspire toward harvests; then the sun lends warmth, the clouds lend rain, the air lends ardor, the soil lends juices. Then must the sower go forth and sow, for nature whispers that if he neglects June he will starve in January.

The planets also lend interpretation to this principle. Years ago our nation sent astronomers to Africa to witness the transit of Venus. Preparations began months beforehand. A ship was fitted up, instruments packed, the ocean crossed, a site selected and the telescopes mounted. Scientists made all things ready for that opportune time when the sun and Venus and earth should all be in line. That critical moment was very brief. Instinctively each astronomer knew that his eye must be at the small end of the glass when the planet went scudding by the large end. Once the period of conjunction had passed no machinery would offer itself for turning the planet back upon her axis. Not for astronomers only are the opportune times brief. For all men alike, failure is blindness to the strategic element in events; success is readiness for instant action when the opportune moment arrives. When nature has fully ripened an opportunity man must stretch out his hand and pluck it. Inventions may be defined as great minds detecting the strategic moment in nature; Galileo finding a lens in the ox's eye; Watt witnessing steam lift an iron lid; Columbus observing an unknown wood drifting upon the shore. To untold multitudes nature offered these opportune moments for discovery, but only Galileo, Watt and Columbus were ready to seize them. As for the rest, this is our only answer to nature: "While thy servant was busy here and there, the strategic moment was gone."

This majestic principle often appears in history. There is a strategy in Providence. Nations, like individuals, have their crisis hours. Through events God makes all society plastic, and then raises up some great man to stamp his image and superscription upon the nation's hot and glowing heart. As scholars move back along the pathway of history, they discern in each great epoch these strategic conditions. How opportune the moment when Jesus Christ appeared!

Alexander's march had scattered every whither the seeds of learning; the Greek language had turned the whole world into one great whispering gallery, in which the nations were assembled; all the provinces around the Mediterranean were linked together by the newly completed system of roads; the Roman judge was in every town to set forth the rights of citizens of the empire; the Roman soldier was there to protect all who brought messages of peace; the long-expected hour had struck. Then Christianity set forth from Bethlehem upon its errand of love. Along every highway ran the eager feet of the messengers of peace and good-will. Events were fully ripe, and soon Christianity was upon the throne of the Caesars.

How strategic that epoch called the fourth century! He who sat in Caesar's palace looked out upon a dying empire. The old race was worn out with war and wine and wealth and luxury. Civilization seemed about to perish, and society was fast sinking back into barbarism. To the north of the Alps were the forest children, ruddy and robust, with their glorious youth full upon them. These young giants needed the dying language and literature and religion, and these great institutions needed their young, fresh blood. But between lay the granite walls builded from sea to sea. Now mark what Charles Kingsley called "the strategy of Providence." Suddenly a blind impulse fell upon the forest children. Two columns started southward. The one rested upon the North Sea and marched southeast; the other rested upon the Ural Mountains and marched southwest; the two met and converged upon Trieste. Without maps or military tactics or plans, wholly ignorant that Napoleon's favorite method of attack was being carried out by them, these two columns converged toward the Alpine pass, and for ten years pounded and pounded against the Roman walls until these yielded and fell. Then the forest children poured down into the vineyards and villages and cities of the dying empire. Multitudes remained to intermarry and preserve the dying race. Other multitudes returned to their old home to sow the northern forests with those great ideas that were to carry civilization through the long night of the dark ages.

Another strategic hour came in the thirteenth century. Then all Europe was stirred with new and awakening life. It was dawn after darkness. Constantinople had fallen and scholars laden with manuscripts went forth to sow Europe with the new learning. The times were fully ripe for another great forward movement for society. Only one thing was lacking--great men for leaders. In that strategic crisis six leaders appeared. God gave each wing of the army of civilization a genius for its general. Copernicus overthrew superstition and brought in science; Luther gave religion, Gutenberg the printing-press, Calvin individualism, Michael Angelo art and the beautiful, Erasmus critical scholarship; and because the old world was filled with debris, and the new ideas needed room, Columbus gave the new world, offering what Emerson calls "the last opportunity of Providence for the human race."

Surely this was a strategic moment in history, giving each citizen unique opportunity.

The strategic element enters into the individual career. Destiny is determined by our use of our critical hours. It is as if life's great issues were staked upon a single throw. Not but that the forces we neglect are permanent. It is that the strategic condition has passed out of them. The sluggard driving his plow into the field in July has sun, soil and seed, but the torrid summer refuses to perform the gentle processes of April. The man who in youth's strategic days denied to memory the great facts of nature and history, in maturer years still has his memory, but the plasticity has gone. It now refuses to hold the facts he gives it. The Latin poet interprets our principle by the story of the maiden in the boat, holding her hand in the water while she toyed with a string of pearls until the string snapped and the treasure sank into the abyss. The miner interprets opportunity lost through him who, for a rifle and a blanket, traded a rich copper mine that has since paid its owner millions. The historian interprets it by Napoleon's bitter signal to his General, tardy at Waterloo, "Too late! the critical hour has passed." Froude interprets it through the old hero bitterly condemning himself over his wife's grave, knowing that his wild love and fierce outburst of affection were impotent now to warm the heart that froze to death in a home.

Ruskin interprets it through a nation that allowed her noblest to descend into the grave, garlanding the tombstone when they refused to crown the brow; paying honors to ashes that were denied to spirit; wreathing immortelles only when they had no use save for laying on a grave where was one dead of a broken heart through a nation's ingratitude. Above all, Jesus Christ interprets it at midnight in Gethsemane, when he saw the torches fluttering in the darkness, heard the clanking of sabers and soldiers' armor, and in sad, reproachful irony wakened his disciples with these words: "Sleep on, now; sleep forever if you will! Henceforth no stress of your vigilance can help me; no negligence of your duty can harm me beyond the harm you have already wrought. Take your ease now. Sleep; the opportunity has gone." Then was the disciples' joy turned into mourning, and for garments of praise did they put on ashes and sackcloth. An irreparable loss was theirs. Yet for all of us each neglected duty means a tragedy. It is always now or never. The treasure wrapped up in each strategic opportunity is of infinite value. To-morrow can hold no joy when yesterday holds this memory: "While I was busy here and there my opportunity was gone."

How strategic the period of youth! Then the chiefest forces of life flow together in sensitive conjunction. Then four great gifts like four great rivers unite in one majestic current to bear up the young man's enterprises, and sweep him on to fame and fortune. Opportune are all the days when health spills over at the eye and ear and laughs through the lips. Men worn out are like overshot wheels--the life trickles and the buckets are filled slowly by long rests and frequent vacations. Young men are like undershot wheels--always, by day and night, the water overflows the banks.

Each morning the young soul wakens to the supreme luxury of living. The world is a great beaker brimmed with wine of the gods. The truth and beauty of field and forest and river give a pleasure that is exquisite to a keenly sensitive and perfectly healthy youth. Like an Aeolian harp, the slightest breath avails for wakening melody midst its strings. But years multiply cares. Age increases heaviness. Time destroys its own children. The poet says: "In youth we carry the world like Atlas; in maturity we stoop and bend beneath it; in age it crushes us to the ground." For the overtaxed and invalided, the dew-drops do not sparkle as diamonds; the wet grass suggests red flannels and cough sirups. For the nervous the bird's song is a meaningless chatter. For the sickly the clouds are big black water-bottles, though time was when they were chariots for God's angels, curtains for hiding ministering spirits trooping homeward at night, leaving all the air sweetly perfumed. It is the body that grants the soul permission to be happy.

To the opportunity offered by health may be added the years lying in front of the young heart like a great estate, as yet unincumbered. Powerful enthusiasms, too, are the inheritance of youth. Noble feelings, fine aspirations then pass through the mind, as in May the perfumed winds from the South pass over the fields. These motives beat upon the mind as steam upon the iron piston. Workmen excavating at Pompeii threw up soil that had been covered for 1,800 years. Exposed to the sun, young trees sprang up. Without the force of light and heat and dew and rain these seeds were dormant or dead. Thus each mind is a dead mind until the full warmth of great impulses quickens the dormant energies. The hopes, the ambitions, the aspirations of youth all conspire to make this a most strategic period. Then all the forces of life unite in a great gulf stream for bearing the soul up and sweeping it forward to new climes and richer shores.

Strategic the hour of prosperity. Men discount the speech of poverty, but the rich man's words weigh a ton each. It has been said that the poor man's dollar is just as good as the rich man's only when both are anonymous, for the dollar with a million behind it will go further than the dollar with a thousand behind it. This is a proverb: "A bid from Rothschild electrifies the market." Each new achievement and success builds higher the tower of observation that lifts the great man into the presence of the nation. All eyes are upon the prospered individual, all ears are alert to his whisper. Prosperity's voice is the voice of an oracle, all her words are winged. Every successful venture in the world of commerce or statecraft quadruples influence over the nation's youth. This principle interprets the curiosity of the boy in store or bank, asking a thousand questions about his successful employer. It explains why the eager aspirant for political influence searches all the journals for some word from Gladstone or Castelar or Bismarck. A sentence from these great champions hath sufficed for reversing the policy of a government. The memory of many triumphs lies back of the great leader's words and lends them weight.

Success is an orator; it charms multitudes. Full oft one who is a veritable genius for making homely truths beautiful has accomplished less for his age than some prosperous man whose few stumbling words have sufficed for shaping national policies and guiding his generation. All the young are drawn into the wake of the successful. Wealth fulfills the story of Orpheus, whose sweet voice made the very stones and trees follow after him. Truly wealth is an evangelist, the almoner of bounty toward college and library and art gallery and liberty and religion. But its chief use is in this: It enables its possessor to repeat his industry, integrity and thrift in the children of a nation. All youthful hearts do well to covet wealth, wisdom and leverage power! But man should remember that the chief value of prosperity is in its capitalization of personality, and the rendering of others sensitive to example and precept. Should man forget this, earth will hear no sadder cry than his when, closing the life career, he exclaims: "While thy servant was busy here and there the opportune moment was gone."

Friendship yields these plastic moments and unique opportunities. For the most part the soul dwells in a castle locked and barred against outsiders. No man can keep open-house for every passer-by. But friendship is an open sesame, drawing every bar and bolt. How the heart leaps when the friend crosses the threshold! His shadow always falls behind him. His coming is summer in the soul; his presence is peace. Friendship glorifies everything it touches. When on a stormy night our friend comes in he seems to warm the very fire upon the hearth; he sweetens the sweet singer's voice; lends new meaning to the wise man's words; gives reminiscence an added charm; makes old stories new; makes the laughter and smiles come twice as often and stay twice as long. Friendship lies upon the heart like a warm fire upon the hearth. By reason of friendship history exhibits every great man as leaving his school of thought and a group of disciples behind him. His spirit lingers with men long after his form has disappeared from the streets, as the sun lingers in the clouds after the day is done, as the melody lingers in the ear long after the song is sung. Longfellow, after a day and a night with Emerson, literally emitted poems and plays. He was stimulated by friendship as bees by rose liquor and the sweet pea wine. Friendship always makes the heart plastic. Then the mental furrows are all open and mellow; sympathy falls like dew and rain; then the heart saith to its friend: "Here am I, all plastic to your touch; work upon me your will; for good or ill--I am thine." Therefore, friendship imposes frightful responsibilities; in asking and receiving it we assume charge of another's destiny. This is the very genius of the teacher's influence over his pupil, the parent's over his child, the general's over his soldier, the patriot's over his people. Better a thousand times never open the furrow than to leave it unfertilized.

How strategic life's better hours! One of God's precious gifts is the luminous hour that denies the lower animal mood. Mind is not always at its best. Full oft our thought is sodden and dull. Then duty seems a maze without a clew and life's skeins all a tangle. The mind is uneasy, confused and troubled. Then men live to the eye and the ear and physical comforts; they live for houses and beautiful things in them; for shelves and rich goods upon them; for factories and large profits by them. Responsibility to God seems like the faint shadow of a vaguely remembered dream. The voice of conscience is in the ear like the far-off murmuring of the sea. The soul is sordid and the finer senses indurated. The angel of the better nature is bondslave to the worst. Then enters some element that nurtures the nobler impulse. Some misfortune, earthquake-like, cleaves through the hard crust. Or some gentle event, like the coming of an old friend or the returning to the old homestead, stirs old memories and kindles new thoughts.

Slowly the heart passes out of the penumbra. The mind, too long obscured like a sun eclipsed by clouds, searches out some rift. Suddenly reason comes into the clear. God rises like an untroubled sun upon the soul's horizon. How crystalline life looks! The mind literally exhales fancies and pictures, and each stick and stone is as full of suggestions and ideas as the forest is full of birds. Old problems become clear as noonday. Difficult questions lie clearly revealed before the mind like landscapes from which the fogs are lifted. Once the mind crawled tortoise-like through its work. Now it soars like an eagle. The soul seems a sweet-spiced shrub, and every leaf is perfumed. If in dull, obscure hours the soul was like a wooden beehive drifted o'er with snow, in its vision-hours the soul is like a glass hive out of which the bees go singing into sweet clover-fields. In these hours how unworthy the material life! How insubstantial the things of iron, wood and stone! Bodily things seem evanescent, as frost pictures on the window on a winter's morn. Then honor, integrity, kindness, generosity alone seem permanent and worth one's while. How easy then to do right. All habits that fettered the faculties like iron cuffs are now felt to be but ice fetters, quickly melting. Then the nobler self, using no whip of cords, looks upon meanness and selfishness, and by a look drives them from the heart and life.

Then years are fulfilled in a single hour. Then from its judgment-seat the soul reviews its past career, searches out secret sins and scorns them. How unworthy are vanity and pride and selfishness. In what garments of beauty and attraction are truth and purity clothed. The soul looks longingly unto the heavenly heights, as desert pilgrims long for oases and springs of water. Unspeakably precious are these strategic hours of opportunity. God sends them; divineness is in them; they cleanse and fertilize the soul; they are like the overflowing Nile. Men should watch for them and lay out the life-course by them, as captains ignore the clouds and headlands and steer by the stars for a long voyage and a distant harbor.

# INFLUENCE, AND THE PRINCIPLE OF REACTION IN LIFE AND CHARACTER.

"So each man gets out of the world of men the rebound, the increase and development of what he brings there. Three men stand in the same field and look around them, and then they all cry out together. One of them exclaims, 'How rich!' another cries, 'How strange!' another cries, 'How beautiful!' And then the three divide the field between them, and they build their houses there, and in a year you come back and see what answer the same earth has made to each of her three questioners. They have all talked with the ground on which they lived, and heard its answers. They have all held out their several hands, and the same ground has put its own gift into each of them. What have they got to show you? One cries, 'Come here and see my barn,' another cries, 'Come here and see my museum;' the other says, 'Let me read you my poem.' That is a picture of the way in which a generation, or the race, takes the great earth and makes it different things to all its children. With what measure we mete to it, it measures to us again. This is the rebound of the hard earth--sensitive and soft, although we call it hard, and feeling with an instant keen discrimination the different touch of each different human nature which is laid upon it. Reaction is equal to action."--*Phillips Brooks*.

To the mystery of life and death must be added the mystery of growth. When Demosthenes exclaimed: "Yesterday I was not here; I shall not be here to-morrow; to-day I am here," he suggested a hard problem. Having solved the enigma, what went before life, and answered that mystery, what follows after death, there still remains this question: "How can a babe in twenty years take on the proportions of the great orator and reformer?" Rocks do not grow, nor diamonds, nor dirt, but a shrunken bulb does become a lily, and a tiny seed a mustard tree. In vain does the scientist struggle with this problem--how an acorn can expand into an oak; how in a single summer a grain of corn can ripen a thousand grains, like that from which the cornstalk sprang.

Men are indeed familiar with the bursting of buds, the cracking of eggs and the growth of children; yet familiarity robs these facts of no whit of their mystery. No jeweler ever goes into the field with a basket of watches to plant them in rows, expecting when autumn hath come to pick two or three wagon-loads of stem-winders from iron branches; yet, were this possible, it would be no more strange than that in the autumn the husbandman should stand under the branches to fill his basket with peaches or bunches of figs. For wise men it is no more difficult to think of a growing engine than of a growing oak. What if to-morrow an engineer should plant a cannon ball. Having watered it well and kept the ground loose through hoe or spade, suppose that when a few weeks have passed the outline of a smokestack should push through the soil, to be followed a little later by a rudimentary steam whistle, the outlines of a boiler, and, rising through the sod, rude drive-wheels, piston-rods and cylinders, until after six months the great engine should stand forth in full completion. This phenomenon would be no more wonderful than that which actually goes on before man's blind eyes, when a tiny seed enlarges into the big tree of California and constructs a vegetable engine that lifts thousands of hogsheads of water up to the topmost boughs without any rattle of chains or the din of machinery.

With difficulty man constructs that musical instrument called a mouthharp, but nature, in six weeks, out of a little blue or brown egg constructs a feathered music-box that automatically conveys itself from tree to tree. But the mystery that has gone on in that tiny blue egg lying in the nest is just as great as if some housewife had planted an old spinning-wheel in the full expectation of reaping a Jacquard loom, or had buried a jew's-harp in the garden expecting in the fall to pick a grand piano. To the mystery that is involved in enlargement by growth must be added the mystery of intelligence. It is not an easy thing for an expert housewife, using the same formula, always to achieve the same happy results in the white loaf. He who plants a strawberry seed will find that the tiny seed will construct a plant, lay in the red tints according to rule and mix the flavor of the berry to a nicety that is the despair of the chef. In the tropic forests there is a flower with a deep cup and the pollen at the bottom. This pollen lies upon a little platter, and underneath the platter is that form of trap known as a figure four, much loved by boys. When the bee, creeping down into the flower, touches that platter, it springs the trap that throws the fertilizing pollen upon the legs of the bee, to be conveyed to the next flower. Wise men can, indeed, imitate this device, but a single seed will in a few months construct many scores of these mechanical devices. To-morrow morning the embryologist in his laboratory will place an egg under a glass cylinder in an atmosphere of 98 degrees. Four hours pass and suddenly the scientist perceives an atom in the heart of that egg give a quick lashing movement. Another moment witnesses two quick throbs. Growth has begun and in four months' time the young eagle with firm strokes will lift itself into the soft air. From the chamber of life and the chamber of death God hath never drawn the curtains. The chamber of growth is another most holy place in which God alone doth stand.

Deeply impressed by the fact of growth, scientists have also marveled at the principle that controls the harvest. Rocks enlarge by accretion, but from what a rock is at the beginning, the geologists cannot tell what will be the shape of that rock when all deposits are finally made. As to growth in seed and shrub, like produces like. He who sows wheat reaps wheat, not tares. He who plants a grape receives a purple cluster, not a bunch of thorns or thistles. He who sows honor shall reap confidence. He who sows frankness shall reap openness. No Peabody sowing industry and thrift reaps the harvest of indolence and idleness. Theodore Parker, loving knowledge and for it denying himself sleep and exercise, reaped wisdom, and also wan and hollow cheeks, while the iron frame and ruddy cheek are for the child of the woods who loves exercise in the open air. He who aspires to leadership and would have the multitude cheer his name, he who longs for the day when his appearance upon the street shall mean an ovation from the people, must make himself the people's slave, defy all demagogues, brave the fury of party strife, oft be execrated by politicians and sometimes be hated by the multitude. Having sown self-sacrifice and love, he shall reap fame and adulation. For nature's law is universal and inexorable--like produces like. The sheaf is simply the seed enlarged and multiplied. The sowing contains the germ of all the harvests to be reaped.

The new biography of Benedict Arnold tells us of the despair of the traitor's final days, the remorse that gnawed his heart, the agony that filled his life. Yet no arbitrary degree was imposed upon Arnold. He plotted the surrender of the interests committed to him as a general, planned the stratagem that ended in the capture and execution of Andre, and received $30,000 in gold for his treachery. Having gone over to the enemy, he placed himself at the head of a band of English troops and went forth to destroy the towns and villages of his boyhood and pillaged the homes of his old friends. He sowed avarice, and of avarice he reaped $30,000. He sowed distrust in America; he reaped distrust from the Englishmen who had bought his honor. He sowed treason; he reaped infamy. He sowed contempt for the colonists, and, dying, he reaped the contempt from his old friends, who counted his body carrion. For the harvests of the soul represent not arbitrary degrees, but the workings of natural law. If Ceres, the goddess of harvests, makes the sheaf to reap the seed, conscience, recalling man's career, ordains that like produces like. What a man soweth that shall he also reap is the law of nature and of God.

The heroes of the Old Testament are common people capitalized. What is unique in the experience of these sons of greatness holds true of all of lesser rank. The career of one of these giants is a pictorial exhibition of this principle of the spiritual harvest. Young Jacob was shrewd, crafty and full of foresight. If Esau, his brother, was a "hail fellow well met," the child of his impulses, Jacob was a diplomat and very wily. One day, when the father, Isaac, was blind and old, Esau grew restless, and at last went away with his companions, for he dearly loved to hunt. In that hour ambition tempted Jacob and avarice led him away. Advantaging himself of his brother's absence, Jacob used the skin of a kid to make his hands hairy, like the hands of Esau, and, simulating the brother's voice, he extorted from his dying father those tokens that, according to the Eastern custom, made him the successor to his father's title, wealth and power. Full twoscore years passed swiftly by and the deceit seems to have brought is large money returns to crafty Jacob.

But silently nature was working out the harvest of retribution, through that law of heredity that makes sons repeat the qualities of their father. When Jacob was now advanced in years his ten sons began, to develop craftiness, and soon they plowed great furrows of care in the father's face. In those days of care his young son Joseph stole into Jacob's heart like a sweet sunbeam, and, with his open, loving ways, filled his father's heart with gladness. When the elder brothers knew Jacob had given Joseph a coat of many colors they remembered the craft of their father in his early career. One evening, when the herds and flocks were scattered widely over the hills, Simeon sent out messengers and called his brothers together for a conference. In that hour he said: "Wist ye not how our father, being a younger son, supplanted his elder brother, Esau? And behold his craft will now make his younger child, Joseph, to supplant his elder brothers! Do ye not remember how our father, Jacob, took a kid and made his hands like unto the hands of Esau? Let us now take a kid and make its blood represent the blood and death of Joseph. What Jacob did for his father, Isaac, let his sons do to their father, Jacob." Thus, with subtle irony, nature made the man's sins to come back to him. A boy, Jacob deceived his father, now, grown gray and old, his boys brought their father an armful of deceits. In that hour when Reuben and Simeon held up the coat of many colors, all red with blood, great nature might have whispered to Jacob: "It is the blood of the kid that you slew for deceiving your father returning to enable your sons to deceive you." For, having sowed deceit, deceit also and stratagem Jacob reaped. Himself a son, he thrust a dart into his father's heart. Become a father, his ten sons became archers, skilled with darts that filled their father's heart with agony. For nature loves justice; her rule is law, sometimes her rod is iron.

The principle that every deed is a seed that contains the germ of its own reward or punishment has received full interpretation by the poets and dramatists. In his "Paradise Lost," Milton has made a detailed study of the principles of the spiritual harvests. The poet represents Satan as an angel, fallen indeed, and sadly battered by his fall, yet still an archangel glorious for strength and beauty. Having visited Paradise and accomplished the destruction of Eve's innocence and Adam's happiness, Satan returns home, passing over a bridge of more prodigious length than now arches the gulf between earth and hell. When the prince arrived at Pandemonium, the capital of Lucifer's realm, he found that the leaders of the fallen host had arranged a reception in the great banquet-hall of the palace. In the presence of the applauding throng, the prince told the story of how he had succeeded in opening the earth as a place to which these exiled angels might retreat from the prison in which they had been so long confined, and pointed to the great bridge spanning the abyss 'twixt earth and hell. When the loud cheerings and rejoicings over this fact had ceased, Satan told by what stratagem he had succeeded in inducing man to break friendship with God. It was not by disguising himself as an angel of light.

But, affirmed Satan, man cared so little for the laws of God that, although disguised as a serpent, he induced man to sin.

> "Then awhile Satan stood, expecting their universal
> shout and high applause
> To fill his ear, when contrary he hears
> On all sides from innumerable tongues
> A dismal universal hiss, the sound
> Of public scorn.  He wondered, but not long
> Had leisure.  Wondering at himself no more,
> His visage drawn, he felt; too sharp and spare
> His arms clung to his ribs, his legs entwining
> Each the other, till supplanted down he fell,
> *A monstrous serpent* on his belly prone,
> *Reluctant, but in vain*.  A greater power
> Now ruled him, *punished in the shape he sinned*,
> According to his doom."

Also when Satan attempted to speak, Milton says, only a hiss went forth "from forked tongue to forked tongue."  When many days had passed by and their hunger was very sore because these fallen angels had seduced man by an apple, it came about that when, fierce with hunger, they seized the fruit ripe upon the branches, the apples were found to be filled with soot and ashes.  By these striking suggestions Milton gives us his idea how angels and men reap what they sow.  Should the literary critic seek an appropriate heading for the tenth book of "Paradise Lost," he could hardly find one more appropriate than this: "What Man Soweth, That Shall He Also Reap."

This law of the spiritual harvest that visits retribution upon unrighteousness or visits reward upon integrity seems to have cast a spell of fascination upon all great writers.  Even those who have written upon liberty, law, patriotism, or love have not been content to end their task until they have, through song or story, illustrated this law of the soul's seedtime and harvest.  The ancient poet who wrote at a time near to the dawn of history makes a strong man go forth to seize his neighbor's flocks and herds, but returning the prince found that in his absence enemies had looted his palace and carried off not only his treasure, but his wife and children. In ending the tale the writer adds the reflection that "God is just!"

Later on the Grecian threw this moral principle into a tale for children, a story that still lives under the title "Baucis and Philemon." One day two travelers entered a village, but as they drew near, each housewife slammed her door, while rude boys threw clods at the wayfarers and let loose their dogs, who snapped and snarled after the travelers. Passing quite beyond the village the pilgrims came to a humble cottage. As they approached his door Philemon came forth to offer refuge, and apologized for the rudeness of his neighbors. The old man prepared for them seats in the grateful shade and hurried to bring them fresh water from the cool spring. Baucis also hastened to bring the loaf, with her one small honeycomb and her pitcher of milk. When the glasses were filled twice and thrice and still the rich milk failed not, the old housewife marveled, until she found that in the bottom of the pitcher there was a fountain from which the rich milk gushed so long as it was needed. Nor did the honeycomb fail, nor did the sharp knife make the wheaten loaf to be less. Having told us that the morning brought disaster to the inhospitable villagers, but brought assurance from these angels who had been entertained unawares that Baucis and Philemon should never more want for earthly goods, the writer of the olden times sets forth for us the principle that good man and bad alike reap what they sow, since each deed contains a harvest like unto itself. Indeed, literature and life teem with exhibitions of this principle. Haman, the rich ruler, builds a gallows for poor Mordecai, whom he hates, and later on Haman himself is hanged upon his own scaffold. David sets Uriah in the front of the battle and robs him of his wife, and when a few years have passed, in turn David is robbed of his wife, his palace also, and his city.

Walter Scott believes in moral retribution. He tells us of a youth who deftly split an arrow at the point where it fitted the bow-string, that when his brother, whom he hated, should bend his bow the arrow might split and, rebounding, pass through his eye. Now it happened that the brother returned from the hunt without using his weapon. That night, alarmed at a commotion without, the youth seized his bow, and, chancing to strike upon that very arrow, was himself slain by the stratagem that he had wickedly planned for his brother. George Eliot, too, has dedicated her greatest volume to the study of this principle. The orphan child, Tito, is received into the arms of an adopted father, who lavishes upon him all his wealth. But when the youth was grown to full strength and beauty, one night Tito left his adopted father in slavery and fled with his gold and gems into a foreign land. Years passed by and, with his stolen wealth, Tito bought wife, palace, position, fame. He had sown falsehood and cruelty, and nothing seemed so unlikely as that he would reap a similar harvest. But one day the people discovered his falsehood and attacked Tito. A mob pursued him through the streets, and, knowing his strength as a swimmer, the youth cast himself into the River Arno. When Tito had swum far down the river to the other side, and, in his exhaustion, would go ashore, he looked up, and, lo! he discerned the gray-haired father whom he had injured trotting along the shore side by side with the swimmer. In the old man's eyes blazed bitter hatred, in his hand flashed a sharp knife. What the youth had sown years before now at last he was to reap. When increasing weakness compelled him to approach the shore he looked beseechingly to his father for mercy, but found only justice. With a wild and bitter cry Tito reaped his harvest. Soon the mud of that river filled the eyes and ears of him who years before had received defilement into his heart. What seed he had sown, that Nature gave him as a harvest--good measure, heaped up, and shaken together.

History permits no man to escape the reflection that if, for the time being, individuals have escaped this moral law, nations have felt its full force. Nature does, indeed, walk through the fields with footsteps so gentle as to disturb no drop of dew hanging upon the blade of grass. Nature also hath her sterner aspect, and for the sons of iniquity her footsteps are earthquakes, her strokes are strokes of war and of pestilence. When Sophocles worked out the law of moral retribution for King Oedipus and Antigone, his daughter, the poet might well have gone on to note that if the Grecian army had sacked the Trojan cities the time would come when the Roman fleet would sack her cities and make her sons to toil as captives. Later on, if the Roman conquerors swept the East for corn and wheat, looted stores and shops, pillaged palaces for treasure for triumphal processions, the time came when Nature and God decreed that the vast wealth piled up in the Roman capital should excite the cupidity of the Goths, until at last the streets of that great city were swept with flame and store-houses were pillaged by marauders. In reviewing the history of

Venice Ruskin was so impressed with this principle of the moral harvest that he affirms that the history of palace and cathedral, of fleets and navies, is simply the story, written by a pen dipped in fire and blood, of how the children reaped what the fathers had sown.

For many months past the statesmen of England have been sending forth discussions reviewing the career of their country. In the light of the Eastern problem one of these authors reflects that whenever England has sown injustice to a weaker nation she has reaped injustice and retribution for herself. He notes that in the last century the governors of England--for example, Lord Hastings--went through the land robbing rajahs, despoiling the people by false weights and measures, until they had turned the whole country into one vast desert. The hour came when before the House of Commons Burke impeached Hastings for high crimes and misdemeanors, as the enemy of India and England and all men. But England was content to impose a trifling fine upon her wicked official. How could she give up the treasure she had filched for herself? Years passed and an injured people brooded upon its wrongs, and the time came when what England had sown in tears she reaped in blood. One day the Indian soldiers mutinied. The next day the wells were filled with the bodies of English officers, their wives and children; then merchants and missionaries and travelers were slaughtered. For weeks the strife went on. If once the English soldier had pillaged the Indian villages, now, in turn, the English quarters were pillaged. "Blind of eye and hard of heart," said the sage statesman. "Retribution hath been visited upon us," said the great leader. "Our jealousy and greed hath ended with that sword being sharpened against ourselves." The note of conviction is in the voice of this statesman, but what saith be save this: "What a man soweth, that also shall he reap!"

All young hearts may well remember that it is safe to do right, but dangerous to sow wrong! No matter how smooth, how soft and sweet, seem the paths of sin, know that beneath every flower there lurks a spider, beneath every silken couch of indulgence there broods a nest of serpents, and the scene that begins with flowers shall end midst thorns and thickets. For the moment, indeed, the judge may seem unobservant and the watchman may seem asleep; but he who yields to any deflection from honor shall find at last that God never slumbers, that his laws never sleep. Go east or go west. Nature is upon the track of the wrong-doer. Could the sage of old sit down to converse with each youth who to-day walks on the street, perchance he would find many who, through excess, are draining away the rich forces of nerve and brain and blood.

Daily they deny reason its book, taste its music, love its noble companionship. At last, when the harp of the physical senses begins to give way, and they fall back upon the mental faculties for pleasure, then these faculties that have been starved shall, in turn, make men suffer. In that hour reason or memory shall say: "Because I called and ye refused; because I stretched out my hand and no man regarded, therefore I will laugh at your calamity. I will mock at your desolation when your fear cometh as destruction and your desolation as whirlwind." In Daniel Webster's words of disappointed ambition, "I still live," we see that a statesman sows what he reaps. In Goethe's fearful cry for "more light" we see that the poet who sows darkness shall reap darkness. In Lord Byron's piteous "I must sleep now" we see that he who sows morbidness and passion reaps feverishness and shame. The law is inexorable. He who sows foul thoughts shall reap the foul countenance of a fiend. He who sows pure thoughts shall reap the sweetness and nobility of the face of Fra Angelico. He who sows reflection shall reap wisdom. He who sows sympathy shall reap love. The good Samaritan who sows tenderness to the man wounded by the wayside shall reap tenderness when angels stoop to bind up his broken heart.

## THE LOVE THAT PERFECTS LIFE.

"Love is the fulfilling of the law."--***Romans, xiii, 10***.

"Men may die without any opinions, and yet be carried into Abraham's bosom, but if we be without love, what will knowledge avail? I will not quarrel with you about opinions. Only see that your heart be right with God. I am sick of opinions. Give me good and substantial religion, a humble, gentle love of God and man."--***John Wesley***.

"Therefore, come what may, hold fast to love. Though men should rend your heart, let them not embitter or harden it. We win by tenderness, we conquer by forgiveness. O, strive to enter into something of that large celestial charity which is meek, enduring, unretaliating, and which even the overbearing world cannot withstand forever! Learn the new commandment of the Son of God. Not to love merely, but to love ***as He loved***. Go forth in this Spirit to your life duties, go forth, children of the Cross, to carry everything before you, and win victories for God by the conquering power of a love like his."--***Frederick W. Robertson***.

The purpose of Christ's mission to earth was the development of ideal manhood. The instruments he fashioned and the agents he ordained all wrought unceasingly toward a manhood that was ample in faculty, fertile in resource and ripe in those qualities that make for maturity of character. He sought to teach men how to carry their faculties through all the strife, collisions and rivalries of life, without damaging men or being damaged by them.

Always to the children of good fortune right living has seemed easy, for these live midst sheltered conditions and exhibit goodness as naturally as the sheltered southern nooks have grass and flowers when all the northern hillsides are brown with death or white with snow. But Christ came teaching the children of weakness and misfortune how to bear up midst adversity, how to sing songs at midnight and how, through defeat, to march to final victory. So beautiful was the manhood he unveiled before men that, beholding it, men low and men high, the publican and prodigal, the centurion and ruler also, quivered with hope, as the harp quivers under the touch of the harper.

For his ideal includes every quality that kindles admiration and delight; all gentleness, all goodness, all simplicity, the refinement of the scholar, the insight of the seer, the courage that makes the youth a hero. In luminous hours men behold visions of ideal perfection hanging like stars in a midnight sky. Unfortunately for many, these visions burst like bubbles and soon pass away. Artists and sculptors look forward to an hour when, by a touch here and a touch there, the statue shall be perfected and the portrait completed; so Christ pointed forward to an hour when, having been wrought upon by darkness and by light, by defeat and by victory, by sorrow and by joy, at last wisdom shall be made perfect, judgment know no error, love have full disclosure and the soul enter into unhindered perfection.

Great are the achievements of the chisel upon the block of marble, marvelous the skill with which a master turns a dead canvas into lustrous life and beauty. Matchless the power that turns a clod into a rosy apple, a seed into a sheaf of wheat, a babe into a sage; yet neither nature nor art knows any transformation like unto that wonder of time when, by slow processes, God develops man out of rude and low conditions of life unto those high and spiritual moods when selfishness gives place to self-sacrifice, coarseness to sweetness, hardness to gentleness and love, and perfection dwells in man as ripeness dwells in fruit, as maturity dwells in harvests.

The mainspring of all progress, individual and social, is the desire to fulfill in character all one has planned in thought. Man's life is one long pursuit of the visions of possible excellence which disquiet, rebuke and tempt him upward. "As to other points," said John Milton, "what God may have determined for me I know not, but this I know--that if he ever instilled an intense love of moral beauty into the breast of any man, he has instilled it into mine. Ceres, in the fable, pursued not her daughter with a greater keenness of inquiry than I, day and night, the idea of perfection." Haunted by his dream of excellence, the poet likened himself to one born beside the throne and reared in purple, yet by some mischance left to gypsies, midst poverty and neglect, while thoughts of the glory he has known and that imperial palace whence he came, are never out of mind. In picturing forth these conceptions of sweetness and light, philosophers have found it hard to summarize the qualities that make up ideal manhood.

Conceding that the Christian is the perfect gentleman, who does for his fellows what an easy chair does for a tired man, what a winter's fire is to a lost traveler, we may also affirm that Newman's definition is inadequate and fragmentary. As the ideal portraits of Christ, from Perugino to Hoffman, divide the kingdom of beauty-- and must be united in one new conception in order to approach the perfect face--so the poets and the philosophers, with their diverse conceptions of ideal manhood, divide the kingdom of character. "The true man cannot be a fragmentary man," said Plato. Is he not one-sided who masters the conventional refinement and the stock proprieties, yet indulges in drunkenness and gluttony? "Pleasure must not be his sole aim," said the accomplished Chesterfield. "I have enjoyed all the pleasures of the world, and consequently know their futility, and do not regret their loss. Those who have no experience are dazzled with there [Transcriber's note: their?] glare, but I have been behind the scenes and have seen all the coarse pulleys, which exhibit and move all the gaudy machines that excite the admiration of the ignorant audience."

Nor is scholarship enough. From Solomon to Burke, the wisest men have been the saddest of men. The Scottish physician who ordered his secretary to select from his library all the books upon medicine and surgery that were printed prior to 1880 and sell them, tells us how futile is the pursuit of wisdom and how rapidly the systems of to-day become the cast-off garments of to-morrow. Nor must the perfect man represent power and wealth alone, for "the wealth of Croesus cannot bring sleep to the sick man tossing upon his silken couch, and all the Alexanders and Napoleons have shed bitter tears, conquering or conquered." He who is merchant or scholar or ruler, and only that, climbs his pillar like Simeon Stylites.

All such know not that the world itself is a pillar all too small for the soul to stand upon. This life-chase after bubbles, this fighting for trifles, this pursuit of false grails, reminds us of the story of that Grecian boy lured to his death by the enchantress. Going into the palace garden to pluck a rose, the youth beheld the form of a young girl standing in the edge of the glimmering woods. With soft words and sweet, she called him. Forgetting his dear ones in the palace, the youth ran after his enchantress. Along a pathway of flowers she danced before him, sometimes sweeping the strings of her harp, sometimes singing, and shaking her curls at his haste, ever shooting arrows from her eyes, yet ever just eluding his embrace. On and on she led him into the bog, that covered his garments with mud, through the thorns and brambles that tore his white skin, over rocks steep and sharp. Ever and anon the youth stopped to pluck the thorns from his hands and bind up his bleeding feet; then, gathering his torn purple about him, he plunged on, in the hope of drinking at last the sweet cup of her sorcery. When, at the end of the day, the desire of his heart was given him, the illusion fell away, for the youth embraced not a beautiful maiden, but an old hag, who had led him into the desert to a hut whose stones were darkness and whose walls were confusion.

As the term genius includes all those forms of culture termed poetry, music, eloquence, leadership, so love is a term that includes all those shapes of human welfare known as education, refinement, liberty, happiness. Properly defined, love is that exalted state of mind and heart when reason is luminous, when judgment and imagination glow under its influence just as the electric bulb glows under the living current. There are three possible states and moods under which the mind may fulfill its functions. There is a dull and quiescent condition when reason and judgment act, but act without fervor. Power is there, but it is latent, just as heat is in the unkindled wood lying on the grate, but the heat is hidden.

Then there is a higher mood of the mind, when, under the influence of conversation or reading, the mind emits jets and flashes of thought, through witticism or story; but this creative mood is intermittent and spasmodic. Last of all is that exalted mood when the mind glows and throbs, when reason emits thoughts, as stars blaze light; when the nimbus that overarches the brows of saints in ancient pictures literally represents the effulgence of the mind. Work done in the lower moods is called mediocre; work done by the mind in the second stage is associated with talent, but when, through birth or ancestry, the mind works ever in regnant and supernal moods, it is called genius. Affirming that all minds rise into this higher mood at intervals, we may also affirm that all the best work in literature or art or commerce has been wrought during these exalted states when love for the work in hand has rendered the mind luminous and crystalline.

It was love of nature that lent Wordsworth his power to divine nature's secret. When the poet approached Chamouni and the mountains that gird it round he tells us he was conscious of a shivering from head to foot, with mingled awe and fear; his mind glowed with an indescribable pleasure; his body thrilled as if in the presence of a disembodied spirit; his heart approached nature with an intensity of joy comparable only to that joy which Dante felt when approaching Beatrice. But when the cares of this world gained upon him and the love of nature faded gradually away in the manner described by him in his "Intimations of Immortality," then also his power to describe nature faded away. For only when the heart loves can intellect do great work.

His biographer tells us that when Angelo grew old and blind he was accustomed to ask his servant to lead him to the torso of Phidias. Passing his hands slowly over the broken marble, the sculptor entered into the thought of the great Grecian, and with love for his art glowing in his face and thrilling in his voice, he mused aloud upon the genius of Phidias. Love of his art made all his days bright and all his moons honeymoons. When Wyatt Eaton, the artist, was in Millet's home he noticed that when the wife called the artist from his task to his noonday meal, the artist's whole being had so gathered itself into the eye that there was no life left with which to hear. Love lent genius skill. No other sentiment is so universal or so powerful in its influence as love that energizes the mind and heart. Love lent swiftness to the feet of Sir Galahad; lent his heart courage; lent his sword victory. Entering the palace, love, said Cicero, "makes gold shine." Love for the birds lent fame to Audubon; just as love for the bees lent fortune to Huber. Love of knowledge hived all the wisdom in the libraries; love of beauty adorned all the galleries; love of service organized all the philanthropies. To-morrow, at the behest of love, and in the interests of dear ones at home, all the wheels will begin to revolve; all the trains go out and all the ships come in. When a man of real force and worth passes upward into that high state of purity and sweet reasonableness called love, he becomes almost sacred and exhales an ineffable and mysterious atmosphere. Great is the power of trade; wonderful the influence of fortune and force; marvelous the hundred instrumentalities and institutions of society, but above all of them is man, whose love can indeed "make riches splendid," whose wisdom love can make mellow, whose strength love can make gentle, whose defeats love can turn into victories. In that hour one hundred men dwell in one man.

Love also perfects morality and fulfills all ethical laws. What health is to the body, what sweetness is to the lark's song, what perfume is to the rose, that morality is to culture and character. Drunkenness and gluttony have not more power to blear the eye than immorality to degrade the soul. When Homer tells us that Ulysses escaped unharmed from the enchanted palace, but suffered injury from his unfaithfulness to a friend, the poet wishes us to know that it is easier to recover from the poison of Circe's cup than to escape the effect of disobedience to the laws of God.

Fortunately nature is so organized as to keep the consequences of ill-doing ever before man's eyes. Disobeying the law of fire man is burned; disobeying the law of steam man is scalded; disobeying the law of honor friends avert their faces, or the door of the jail closes behind the wrongdoer. So few are these laws and so simple that they could not be plainer were they emblazoned upon the sky as an ever-present scroll. There is the law of reverence. Conscious of vastness and sublimity, in the presence of mountains, man, frail, ignorant, passing swiftly to his grave, is asked to bow his head in the presence of the Eternal One.

There is also the law of truth in speech, the law of purity in thought, the laws that forbid theft and covetousness and killing. But all these laws are gathered up and fulfilled in love, just as the seven colors of nature are gathered up and fulfilled in the one white sunbeam. And he who loves will fulfill all these laws. Loving himself, man will not waste his physical treasure. As it was vandalism for the iconoclasts to pass through the cathedrals of Europe whitewashing the frescoes and breaking down the statues, much more is it vandalism for men to destroy that temple of God called the body. If man loves his mind he will, through culture, lead what is germinal and latent forth into full blossom and fruitage. He who loves scholarship will make haste to double the books in his library. He who loves sweetness will double the sweetness of his melody. He who loves friends will double their number and strengthen their affection. He who loves industry will strengthen his toil and lend it influence. Looking toward the home, love fulfills the law of helpfulness. Looking toward the weak and poor, love fulfills the law of service and sympathy. Looking toward a great crisis for humanity, love fulfills the law of martyrdom.

Just as summer fulfills all ripeness and growth for seed and root and tree, so love fulfills all laws for self and man and the all-loving God.

After thirty-six years of tireless toil Herbert Spencer has brought to a conclusion the labors of a lifetime. His final volume places the capstone on the structure of his philosophy. In reading these pages no thoughtful mind can fail to perceive that for science also has dawned the vision splendid. If history began with an era of force, its last and crowning achievement will be the era when love, organized into laws and institutions, will lend perfection to civilization. The upward march of mankind has been slow and accompanied by tremendous losses. At the beginning strength prevailed and weakness went to the wall; the bird with the swiftest wing first reached the fountain, the deer with the swiftest foot reached the place of shelter, the ox with the strongest thrust reached the richest fodder. Pushed back, weakness perished, while strength prevailed and propagated.

This law of violence received its first check through the parental instinct. Parenthood built a fortress with walls and bulwarks about the babe. Love of offspring caused a weakness to survive. At last an era dawned when many parents united to construct a shield for weak children indeed, but also for weak adults. The state lifted the shield between weakness and its oppressor. The widow and the orphan were permitted to glean after the harvesters. The traveler, passing through the field, might pluck a handful of corn or pull a bunch of figs. The creditor must not take the blanket or coat from the laborer nor the boat from the poor fisherman, nor the plane or saw from the poor carpenter. Stimulated by Christ's example and teachings, society began to multiply the bulwarks against tyranny and selfishness. Looking toward the child, for the protection of weakness and unripeness, the state built these shields called the school and library, looking toward the unfortunate and those weak in body or mind, the state built bulwarks called asylum and hospital. Looking toward the chimney-sweep, the factory boys and girls, the state began to soften pain and mitigate the distress of labor. Looking toward the serf and the slave and the prisoner, the novelist and poet constructed song and story as shields for the protection of the weak and the oppressed.

One hundred years ago a man was as a beast of the field, and the slaughter of men in Italy, by the tyrant who ruled over them, stirred no more thought in England than the news of the slaughter of so many beasts. But fifty years ago the state had become so gentle toward the weak that when Mr. Gladstone made a protest against the savagery and infuriated cruelty wrought upon the inmates of the dungeons of Italy, then the heart of Europe turned toward Rome, the throne trembled upon its foundations. Formerly when any foreign government wished to colonize Africa, they sent out a regiment of soldiers, cut off a slice of the country and annexed it. Now public sentiment forbids such tyranny. The only way the aggressive nations can obtain possession of new territory is to do it under the name of a protectorate, sugar-coating, as has been said, the deeds of tyranny. If the dungeon has been rifled of its prey, if cruelty has been scourged out of the land, if despotism tottered, it is because society was slowly climbing up that stairway, of which the first step is fear and the last is love.

In these January days our earth, snow-clad and frost-bound, seems like a huge ball of ice. Yet all unconsciously to itself, the earth is being swept on into spring and summer. Unconsciously, but none the less truly, society, under the silent and secret impulse of the great God, has been journeying upward toward the time when love shall fulfill every law; when kindness and sympathy shall be organized in manners and customs. All the revolutions of the past, all the clangor of war, all the tumbling down of Bastilles, all the piling up of cities, is as nothing to the advance of the world toward that era when love shall perfect man's institutions and civilization.

Love also perfects religion. It is the glory of Christ that he unveils the sovereignty of character and crowns manhood with all-maturing and all-perfecting love. Looking backward, man finds that all religions fall into four classes: There is the religion of fear and force, when man offers sacrifices to appease the gods and conciliate justice. There is the religion of law, when men reduce life to formal rules, and the Pharisee rigorously fulfills his duty as chief, or trader, or friend. There is the religion of romanticism, when men of powerful intellect and strong imagination evolve their ideal and, withdrawing to some cave, give themselves to reverie. In all such self becomes an orb, so large as to eclipse brother man and God. Last of all there is the religion of Christ, in which love is root, blossom and fruitage. It aims at the development and unfolding of everything that is gracious in life, whatever strikes at admiration, whether it is in school, in art, in song, in wit, in travel, in books; whatever is praiseworthy in courage or endurance, whatever has fineness and sweetness and nobility; all that belongs to the hero and patriot; all that belongs to the seer and scholar; all that belongs to leadership in trade and commerce--all these elements are to be united and carried upward into the sweetness and purity of life, until the full man, standing apart and standing above life, seems to have been informed with divine love, as with a presence.

And when love has made the most of the man himself it overflows to bless others. Christ's disciples are not here to be ministered unto, but to minister. Religion, says Christ, is love, and love is gentle toward those with hollow eyes and famine-stricken faces. Love is kindly toward those who have a tragedy written in the sharpened countenance. Love is patient toward those who have lost fidelity, as a man loses a golden coin; who have lost morality as one who flounders in the Alpine drifts. And this religion of love takes on a thousand modern forms. If it is not rowing out against the darkness and storm, as did Grace Darling to save the shipwrecked, it is going forth to those tossed upon life's billows, to succor and to save. For love is making the individual life beautiful, making the home beautiful, and will at last make the church and state beautiful. Men will not bow down to crowned power nor philosophic power nor esthetic power; but, in the presence of a great soul, filled with vigor of inspiration and glowing with love, man will do obeisance. There is no force upon earth like divine love in the heart of man, and at last that force will sweeten and regenerate society.

Love also fulfills immortality. Of late science has reduced the number of things that endure. The astronomer tells us the sun is burning up, and will be a dying ash-heap as truly as the coal in man's cellar will be exhausted. The geologists tell us the flowing of "the crystal springs wearies the mountain's heart as truly as the beating of the crimson pulse wearies man's; that the force of the iron crag is abated in its time, like the strength of human sinews in old age." The everlasting mountains are doomed to decay as surely as the moth and worm. It seems that the shining texture of stars and suns must wax old, like a garment, and decay. If now youth is eager to master all knowledge, plunge into the thick of life's battle, forge some tool, enact some law, right some wrong, the time will speedily come when the man will sit down amid the ruins of his life and confess that his idols have been shivered, one by one.

He who loves endures. For him always all is well. That youth with a great love for nature's treasures that promised fame, but who found his open book crimson with the life-current, may dry his tears, for love is immortal and beyond he will fulfill the dreams denied here. Because he loves the slave, Livingstone, falling in the African forest, need not fear, for love will make his work immortal. The sweet mother, whose love overarches the cradle with thoughts that for number are beyond the stars, need not fear to leave behind the gentle babe, for everlasting love will encircle it. Falling into unconsciousness and putting out upon the yeasty sea midst the falling darkness, man may call back: "I still live." For God is love and God is eternal. Therefore man who loves is immortal also.

# HOPE'S HARVEST, AND THE FAR-OFF INTEREST OF TEARS.

"Let Love clasp Grief lest both be drown'd,
Let Darkness keep her raven gloss;
Ah, sweeter to be drunk with loss,
To dance with Death to beat the ground!"-- *Tennyson*.

"Soul, rule thyself. On passion, deed, desire,
Lay thou the laws of thy deliberate will.
Stand at thy chosen post. Faith's sentinel:
Though Hell's lost legions ring thee round with fire,
Learn to endure. Dark vigil hours shall tire
Thy wakeful eyes; regrets thy bosom thrill;
Slow years thy loveless flower of youth shall kill;
Yea, thou shalt yearn for lute and wanton lyre.
Yet is thy guerdon great; thine the reward
Of those elect, who, scorning Circe's lure,
Grown early wise, make living light their lord.
Clothed with celestial steel, these walk secure,
Masters, not slaves. Over their heads the pure
Heavens bow, and guardian seraphs wave God's sword."-- *V. A. Symonds*.

The soul is monarch of three kingdoms. Man lives at once in the present, the past and the future. Memory presides over yesterday; to-day is ruled by reason; to-morrow is under the sway of hope. The ancient seer who stood by the historic vine reflecting how the rain of yesterday had disappeared to give its sweet liquors to the roots only to reappear to-morrow in purple

clusters, gave us a beautiful image of himself. Each human life is like unto a vine-
-its trunk manifest in the present; its roots deeply buried in the past; its branches
throwing themselves forward, ripening fruit for days to come. Life is a solid column
of days all compacted together. To-day's usefulness is in the number of wise, happy
and helpful yesterdays, whose accumulated treasures crowd forward the soul's present activities. But for his yesterdays stored up in memory man would be impotent
for any heroic thought or deed. He would remain a perpetual infant. As the child
journeys away from the cradle memory gathers up and carries forward faces, words,
books, arts, sciences, literatures, and these recollections are embalmed and trans-
mitted as soul-capital, legacies unspeakably precious.

Yesterday, therefore, is no mausoleum of dead deeds; no storehouse of mum-
mies. Memory is a granary holding seed for to-morrow's sowing; memory is an
armory holding weapons for to-morrow's battles, memory is a medicine-chest with
balms for to-morrow's hurts; memory is a library with wisdom for to-morrow's
emergency. Yesterday holds the full store of to-day's civilization, contains our
tools, conveniences, knowledges; contains our battlefields and victories; above all
gives us Bethlehem and Calvary. But alone man's yesterday is impotent; his to-
morrow insufficient. The true man binds all his days together with an earnest, intense, passionate purpose. His yesterdays, to-days and to-morrows march together,
one solid column, animated by one thought, constrained by one conspiracy of desire, energizing toward one holy and helpful purpose, to serve man and love God.

God governs man through the regency of hope. The reasons thereof are self-
evident. Man is born a long way from home. No cradle rocks a full-orbed manhood. The babe begins a mere handful of germs; a bough of unblossomed buds.
It is a weary climb from nothing to manhood, at its best. As things rise in the
scale of being the distance between birth and maturity widens. Mollusks are born
close up to their full estate, sandflies mature in two days, butterflies in two weeks,
humming-birds in as many months. But let no man think the vast all-shadowing
redwood trees of California grew in a mushroomic night. When the seed first thrust
its rootlets down into the soil and its plumule up to the sunshine it entered upon a
long career. Saved by hope after 800 years of growth it gives shade to myriads of
birds; beams for lath and loom and ship in the service of industry; lends pen and
pencil to poet and artist in the service of beauty; through desk and pew enters into

man's intellectual and moral life; through instruments of convenience strengthens the sweet amenities of the home; working, it also waited and is saved by hope.

Man stands at the very summit of creation. He is at the head of all that creep and swim and walk and fly. Preparatory to his dominion he begins with the lowest and runs the whole gamut of experience of all living things below him. And hope alone can save him as he journeys upward through all the intermediate stages on his way to his throne and his God. Big with destiny, he is saved by hope. Not to-day and not yesterday can suffice. The present offers only standing room--four-and-twenty hours. Memory is a bin banked with snowdrifts, not the waving harvest-fields. Man's life is all in front of him. His large endowment asks for an extended period of time, asks seventy years for skill toward his body; asks an immortal destiny for mind and heart. He is saved by hope and futurity.

Consider the scope and functions of hope and aspiration. Man is governed from above and within; while rocks, birds, beasts are governed from below and without. Gravity holds the bowlder in its place. The channel saith to the river: "Thus far and no farther." The fawn that is struck, the lion that strikes, the eagle dwelling above both, are controlled by fear. The charioteer drives his steeds from behind and controls by rein and scourge. But man is controlled from within and in front. God does not scourge his children forward through whips of fear. Hopes moving on before him lure him onward. The Italian artist shows us the child passing near the precipice. Then drew near a gentle guardian spirit. The unseen friend rolled along the pathway apples of Paradise and the child, following after with shouts of glee, was lured from danger. To the beauty of the artist's thought Homer's story adds elements of instruction. When the Grecian boy was pursued by a giant whose breath was fire, whose hand held a huge club, two invisible beings lent help. One took the boy's hand and lifted him forward, the other casting an invisible cord over him flew before him until his speed was doubled and the palace gates gave shelter. Oh, beautiful story of God's gentle rule o'er men! When troubles sweep over the world like sheeted storms, when men fear exceedingly and strong men cower and shrink and little ones believe the next step to be the precipice, then God smiles. Striking some sweet bell he sends forth messengers to lure men forward; they hang stars in man's night; they whisper that the twilight is nothing, since it is morning twilight; that fears are bats and owls hooting at the dawn; that hope is a lark singing the new day; that God reigns and all is well. Then depart all fears and superstitions. The courage of the future comes; the columns begin a forward march. These upward movements of society are the yearnings of God's heart lifting his children forward by hope.

Hope and aspiration also furnish the secret springs of civilization. All things useful and beautiful were once only hopes and ideas. Free institutions are ideals of liberty, crystallized into word forms. Tools and instruments are ideals dressed up in iron clothes. The early forest man dwelt in a cave; ached with cold and moaned with hunger. Going into the forest to dig roots he found honey hived by the bees and nuts stored up by squirrels against the winter. Straightway hope suggested to him a larger granary, whence hath come all man's bins and storehouses. Man plucked a large plum and found it sour, and another plum small, but sweet. Hope suggested that he unite the two and strike through the abundant acid juices of the one with the sugar of the other. Thence came all vineyards and orchards. Digging in the soil tired him, but hope suggested that his pet ox might pull his forked stick; when the wooden stick wore blunt hope replaced it with an iron point; when the iron point refused to scour hope suggested steel; when the steel made his burden light and doubled the pace of his steeds, hope suggested a seat on the plow; when the riding-plow gave him time to think, hope suggested he could increase the harvest by doubling the depth, when the weight was overheavy for his beasts, hope suggested a steam-plow. The Kensington Museum exhibits the growth of the plow idea, as it moved from the forked stick to the "steam gang." If in this procession of material plows we could see the procession of ideal plows we would find that thoughts and hopes are a thousandfold more than material things.

By hope also do the people increase in wisdom and culture and character. Millions of men are digging and toiling twelve hours each day; and God hath sent forth hope to emancipate them from drudgery. The man digging with his pick hath a far-away look as he toils. Hope is drawing pictures of a cottage with vines over the doorway, with some one standing at the gate, a sweet voice singing over the cradle. Hope makes this home his; it rests the laborer and saves him from despair. Multitudes working in the stithy and deep mines sweeten their labor and exalt their toil by aspiring thoughts. Thinking of his little ones at home, the miner says: "My children shall not be as their father was; my drudgery is not for self, but for love's sake; the sweat of my brow is oil in the lamp of love; I will light it to-night on the sacred altar of home." Here is the secret of the rise and reign of the people. This explains all man's progress in knowledge and culture. As the fruits and flowers rise rank upon rank in response to the advancing summer, so all that is most refined and exalted in man's mind or heart bursts forth in new ideals, reforms, revolutions, in response to the revelation of that personal presence from whom all hope and aspiration incessantly proceed.

Hope's noble ministry hath grievous enemies. Among these let us include a false use of the past. Yesterday contains sins and mistakes, but multitudes err in dwelling too much upon their wrongs. Each man hath had his temptations, each his fierce conflicts and defeats, each bears grievous scars from the battle-field. Yet if one constantly revives all his old sins life will be filled with hideous specters. Memory will become a place of torment and a ghastly chamber of horrors. We shall be the children of despondency and wretchedness. Memory will be a graveyard; the past will give no light save the "will-o-the-wisp" light from putrescence and decay. All the springs of joy will be poisoned by morbid griefs that keep open old wounds. The city hath its offal heap where refuse matter is destroyed; each home its garret, the contents cast out at regular intervals; the individual throws away his old clothes, old tools, old vehicles. Why should not the soul have its refuse valley--where the past is cast out of life and memory?

Farmers' boys sometimes set steel traps by shocks of corn whither come quail and prairie chickens. Stepping upon the traps, the cruel jaws close upon foot or wing and the bleeding bird beats out its life upon the frozen ground. Memory often with cruel jaws holds men entrapped. A single error wrecks the whole life. But once forgiven of God let the sin go. Reflection upon past sins is good only so long as it produces revulsion from sin, and like a bow shoots the soul toward God and righteousness. God is like a mother who forgives the child's sin into everlasting forgetfulness. Man should be ashamed to remember what God forgets. "I will cast your sins into the depth of the sea." Someone says: "God receives the soul as the sea the bather, to return it cleansed--itself unsoiled." Gather up, therefore, all thy sins--old wrongs, old hatreds, burning angers, memories of men's treachery; stuff them into a bag and heave them into the gulf of oblivion. Your life is not in the past, but in the future. "We are saved by hope."

Multitudes may embitter their new year by undue reflections over opportunities neglected and lost in the past and denied in the present. Professor Agassiz tells of a friend who sold his farm in Pennsylvania for $5,000 to invest it in Dakota, and after losing all in the new home returned to find the German who purchased the homestead had found oil and great wealth in a swamp which he had tried to drain off.  An old gentleman recently told of his refusal in 1840 to accept as payment of a small note a lot on a corner in Chicago now worth a million dollars, and he shed bitter tears over the loss of property he never owned. When Ali Hafed heard of the diamonds in India he sold his estate and went forth to seek his fortune.  His successor, watering his camel in the garden, saw the gleam of gems in the white sand and discovered the Golconda mines.  Had Ali Hafed had eyes to see his would have been boundless treasure at home instead of poverty, starvation and death. These and similar legends stand for the opportunities that have gone forever.  How many neglected their opportunities for education; how they knocked unbidden at every door and no man opened.  Others were denied culture, and now feel they are unfulfilled prophecies.  Many by one error have injured eye or ear or lung or limb or nervous system. They grievously handicapped themselves.  Others by ingratitude, infidelity to trusts, treachery to friends, have poisoned happiness. Repentance is theirs, and also forgiveness, but not forgetfulness.  The past is full of bitterness.

Let the dead past bury its dead.  The future is still ours.  The trees in October willingly let go their leaves to fall into the ditch.  Their life is not in last year's leaves, but in the infant buds that crowd the old leaves off.  Put forth new activities.  Open new furrows.  Sow new seed.  All the tomorrows are thine; but they are few and short. Fulfill his dictum who said: "I am as one going once across this vast continent; I would lean forth and sow as far as hand can scatter my seed.  Let the angels count the bundles."  No man should be discouraged in whom God believes, preserving him in life.  Let hope in God sweeten life's bitterness.

Another enemy of hopefulness is found in nervous excesses and overwork. Men drain away their vitality. Ambitions unduly stimulate the brain. Many break the laws of sleep and the laws of digestion and the laws of nerve sobriety.  They spend their brain capital.  Then they grow hopeless toward home and business. Ill-health spreads a gloom over all life.  Every judgment is pessimistic; it could not be otherwise.  The jaundiced eye yellows the landscape.  The sweetest music rasps like a file upon the nervous ear. Thomas Carlyle's pessimism was largely physical. He overworked upon his life of Oliver Cromwell. Maurice once said: "Carlyle believed in God down to the time of Oliver Cromwell." Once, in a moment of depression, Lyman Beecher prayed: "Lord, keep us from despising our rulers, and help them to stop acting so we cannot help despising them." Poor, nerve-racked Pascal, grew fearful lest his affection for his sister, who had nursed him through a long illness, was sinful. One day he wrote in his journal: "Lord, forgive me for loving my dear sister so much!" Afterward he drew his pen through the word "dear." Hope and trust toward God go with health. Sickliness is not saintliness. God cannot save by hope what man destroys by ill-health.

Dean Stanley used hopefulness as a test of all systems of truth. Rightly so. God is the God of hope, and his truth, like himself, carries the atmosphere of good cheer. The falsity of medievalism appears in this--it robbed men of joy and gladness. God was the center of darkness. His throne was iron. His heart was marble. His laws were huge implements of destruction. His penalties were red-hot cannon balls crashing along the sinner's pathway. Repentance toward God was moving toward the arctics and away from the tropics. Christianity was anything but "peace on earth, good will to men."

Philosophers destroyed God's winsomeness. The reformers came in to lead men away from medievalism back to God himself. Men found hope again in redemptive love. They saw that any conception of God that dispirited and depressed men was perverted and false. No man hath done more to establish this fact than him who long ago said: "Any presentation of the gospel of Jesus Christ that does not come to the world as the balmy days of May comes to the unlocked northern zones; any way of preaching the love of God in Christ which is not as full of sweetness as the voice of the angels when they sang at the advent; any way of making known the proclamation of mercy which has not at least as many birds as there are in June and as many flowers as the dumb meadows know how to bring forth; any method of bringing before men the doctrine of salvation which does not make everyone feel, 'There is hope for me in God--in the divine plan, in the very nature of the organization of human life and society,' is spurious--is a slander on God and is blasphemy against his love."

Hope hath her harvest also for teachers and reformers. Often men think their work is squandered. They seem to be sowing seed not upon the Nile, to find it again abundantly, but in midocean, to sink and come to naught. Parents and teachers break their hearts, fearing their watchfulness and instruction have failed. Men sow wheat and wait six months for a harvest; but they sow moral seed Sunday and on Monday whip their children because the seed has not ripened. They forget that apples bitter in July may be sweet in August. To-day's vice in the child is often to-morrow's virtue, as acid juices through frost become saccharine. Yesterday the mother rocked a little angel in the cradle; to-day she moans: "Alas, that I should have rocked a little fox, a little serpent, a little wolf!" To-morrow the child becomes a model of truth and integrity.

The sage might have said: "It is good that woman should hope and wait." Truth's errand has always been a successful errand. Not a single social truth or civic truth or moral truth has ever been lost out of the world. Secrets of cruelty and fraud, secrets of oppression and sin perish, but nothing that makes life happier or better hath been forgotten. We do not have to keep God and truth alive, they keep us alive. Vegetable seeds can be killed, but not moral seeds. When God issues his silent command to the earth flying into winter and wheels it back toward summer, it is given to no man to put a brake upon warmth; nor can he go up against the spring with swords and banners. But easier this than staying the upward march of mankind. God is abroad upon a mission of recovery. Open thy hand, O publicist! and sow thy seed. The seed shall perish, but not the harvest.

Our childhood was pleased with the story of the old monk who was shipwrecked alone on a desert isle. He always carried with him a few roots and seeds. Planting these, he died, but sailors coming twenty years later found the isle waving with fruit trees. To the beauty of this legend let us add the truth of one who has made all this land his debtor. In 1801 a youth passed through western Pennsylvania. He was collecting apple seeds with which to found orchards in the then unbroken states of Ohio, Indiana, Illinois and Michigan. When he came to an open, sunny spot in the forest he would plant his seeds and protect them with a brush fence. Years afterward new settlers found hundreds of these embryo orchards in the forests. Thrice he floated his canoe laden with seeds down the Ohio to the settlers in Kentucky. To this brave man, called by our Congressional Record "Johnny Appleseed," whole states owe their wealth and treasure of vineyards and orchards.

This intrepid man is a beautiful type of all those who, passing through life's wastes, sow the land with God's eternal truths, whose leaves and fruits heal nations. If God remembers the roots in dark forests he will not forget his truths in human hearts. Therefore, sow thy seed. Ye are saved by hope.

The ground and basis of all hope whatsoever is God. It is his good providence and redemptive love in Jesus Christ that make us optimists. Hope is not within the scope of our wisdom or culture or skill; and hope is not in our health or tool or treasure. We journey into an unknown future. It is not given to us to know what a day or an hour of the new year may bring forth. How impotent are the wisest and strongest in the hour when we hear the sound of the ocean and in darkness ford the deep and dangerous river, beyond which is high and eternal noon. What can the child on some great ocean steamer caught in a winter's storm do to overcome the tempest? Can it drive the fierce blasts back to their northern haunts? Can its little hand hold the wheel and guide the great ship? Can its voice still the billows that can crush the steamer like an egg-shell? Can its breath destroy the icy coat of mail that covers all the decks? What the child can do is trust the Captain who has brought this same ship through a hundred hard storms. It can rest and trust and hope. And all we upon this great earth-ship have been caught, not in a storm, but in the gulf stream of God's providence. The warm tropic currents sweep us on to the heavenly harbor. The trade winds above aid the forward flight. More than all else is the larger planetary movement that sweeps gulf stream, winds and ship onward towards the infinite. Soon shall we enter into quiet waters and cast out our anchor.

Looking forward, let us hope and cleanse all fear out of life--trust God, love him and rejoice. Even our largest problems need not dispirit us. Problems are not to be analyzed, but accepted. He who analyzes a flower loses it. He who cracks a diamond to see what it is, is without both gem and knowledge. Life's great questions are seeds. Plant a seed, then wait. Some day the flower and fruit will explain the seed. It is well to lay aside difficult questions to be asked some day at the throne of God. Then we will look back to smile at what now disturbs us exceedingly. Remember the Russian Cathedral--travelers tell us the din and noise of the crowds thronging under the dome to those above the dome become a strain of soft music. It is good to hope and wait. Because God lives and loves, man should enter the future as he enters temple or cathedral--to dedicate all its days to hope and aspiration.

### The Codes Of Hammurabi And Moses
### W. W. Davies

QTY

The discovery of the Hammurabi Code is one of the greatest achievements of archaeology, and is of paramount interest, not only to the student of the Bible, but also to all those interested in ancient history...

**Religion**    **ISBN: *1-59462-338-4***    **Pages:132**
*MSRP $12.95*

### The Theory of Moral Sentiments
### Adam Smith

QTY

This work from 1749. contains original theories of conscience amd moral judgment and it is the foundation for systemof morals.

**Philosophy  ISBN: *1-59462-777-0***    **Pages:536**
*MSRP $19.95*

### Jessica's First Prayer
### Hesba Stretton

QTY

In a screened and secluded corner of one of the many railway-bridges which span the streets of London there could be seen a few years ago, from five o'clock every morning until half past eight, a tidily set-out coffee-stall, consisting of a trestle and board, upon which stood two large tin cans, with a small fire of charcoal burning under each so as to keep the coffee boiling during the early hours of the morning when the work-people were thronging into the city on their way to their daily toil...

**Pages:84**

**Childrens  ISBN: *1-59462-373-2***    *MSRP $9.95*

### My Life and Work
### Henry Ford

QTY

Henry Ford revolutionized the world with his implementation of mass production for the Model T automobile. Gain valuable business insight into his life and work with his own auto-biography... "We have only started on our development of our country we have not as yet, with all our talk of wonderful progress, done more than scratch the surface. The progress has been wonderful enough but..."

**Pages:300**

**Biographies/    ISBN: *1-59462-198-5***    *MSRP $21.95*

www.bookjungle.com *email: sales@bookjungle.com fax: 630-214-0564 mail: Book Jungle PO Box 2226 Champaign, IL 61825*

## The Art of Cross-Examination
## Francis Wellman

QTY

I presume it is the experience of every author, after his first book is published upon an important subject, to be almost overwhelmed with a wealth of ideas and illustrations which could readily have been included in his book, and which to his own mind, at least, seem to make a second edition inevitable. Such certainly was the case with me; and when the first edition had reached its sixth impression in five months, I rejoiced to learn that it seemed to my publishers that the book had met with a sufficiently favorable reception to justify a second and considerably enlarged edition. ..

Pages:412

Reference     ISBN: *1-59462-647-2*          MSRP $19.95

## On the Duty of Civil Disobedience
## Henry David Thoreau

QTY

Thoreau wrote his famous essay, On the Duty of Civil Disobedience, as a protest against an unjust but popular war and the immoral but popular institution of slave-owning. He did more than write—he declined to pay his taxes, and was hauled off to gaol in consequence. Who can say how much this refusal of his hastened the end of the war and of slavery ?

Law          ISBN: *1-59462-747-9*          Pages:48

MSRP $7.45

## Dream Psychology Psychoanalysis for Beginners
## Sigmund Freud

QTY

Sigmund Freud, born Sigismund Schlomo Freud (May 6, 1856 - September 23, 1939), was a Jewish-Austrian neurologist and psychiatrist who co-founded the psychoanalytic school of psychology. Freud is best known for his theories of the unconscious mind, especially involving the mechanism of repression; his redefinition of sexual desire as mobile and directed towards a wide variety of objects; and his therapeutic techniques, especially his understanding of transference in the therapeutic relationship and the presumed value of dreams as sources of insight into unconscious desires.

Pages:196

Psychology     ISBN: *1-59462-905-6*          MSRP $15.45

## The Miracle of Right Thought
## Orison Swett Marden

QTY

Believe with all of your heart that you will do what you were made to do. When the mind has once formed the habit of holding cheerful, happy, prosperous pictures, it will not be easy to form the opposite habit. It does not matter how improbable or how far away this realization may see, or how dark the prospects may be, if we visualize them as best we can, as vividly as possible, hold tenaciously to them and vigorously struggle to attain them, they will gradually become actualized, realized in the life. But a desire, a longing without endeavor, a yearning abandoned or held indifferently will vanish without realization.

Pages:360

Self Help          ISBN: *1-59462-644-8*          MSRP $25.45

**The Rosicrucian Cosmo-Conception Mystic Christianity** *by Max Heindel*   ISBN: *1-59462-188-8*   **$38.95**
*The Rosicrucian Cosmo-conception is not dogmatic, neither does it appeal to any other authority than the reason of the student. It is: not controversial, but is: sent forth in the, hope that it may help to clear...*   New Age/Religion Pages 646

**Abandonment To Divine Providence** *by Jean-Pierre de Caussade*   ISBN: *1-59462-228-0*   **$25.95**
*"The Rev. Jean Pierre de Caussade was one of the most remarkable spiritual writers of the Society of Jesus in France in the 18th Century. His death took place at Toulouse in 1751. His works have gone through many editions and have been republished...*   Inspirational/Religion Pages 400

**Mental Chemistry** *by Charles Haanel*   ISBN: *1-59462-192-6*   **$23.95**
*Mental Chemistry allows the change of material conditions by combining and appropriately utilizing the power of the mind. Much like applied chemistry creates something new and unique out of careful combinations of chemicals the mastery of mental chemistry...*   New Age Pages 354

**The Letters of Robert Browning and Elizabeth Barret Barrett 1845-1846 vol II**   ISBN: *1-59462-193-4*   **$35.95**
*by Robert Browning and Elizabeth Barrett*
Biographies Pages 596

**Gleanings In Genesis (volume I)** *by Arthur W. Pink*   ISBN: *1-59462-130-6*   **$27.45**
*Appropriately has Genesis been termed "the seed plot of the Bible" for in it we have, in germ form, almost all of the great doctrines which are afterwards fully developed in the books of Scripture which follow...*   Religion/Inspirational Pages 420

**The Master Key** *by L. W. de Laurence*   ISBN: *1-59462-001-6*   **$30.95**
*In no branch of human knowledge has there been a more lively increase of the spirit of research during the past few years than in the study of Psychology, Concentration and Mental Discipline. The requests for authentic lessons in Thought Control, Mental Discipline and...*   New Age/Business Pages 422

**The Lesser Key Of Solomon Goetia** *by L. W. de Laurence*   ISBN: *1-59462-092-X*   **$9.95**
*This translation of the first book of the "Lernegton" which is now for the first time made accessible to students of Talismanic Magic was done, after careful collation and edition, from numerous Ancient Manuscripts in Hebrew, Latin, and French...*   New Age/Occult Pages 92

**Rubaiyat Of Omar Khayyam** *by Edward Fitzgerald*   ISBN:*1-59462-332-5*   **$13.95**
*Edward Fitzgerald, whom the world has already learned, in spite of his own efforts to remain within the shadow of anonymity, to look upon as one of the rarest poets of the century, was born at Bredfield, in Suffolk, on the 31st of March, 1809. He was the third son of John Purcell...*   Music Pages 172

**Ancient Law** *by Henry Maine*   ISBN: *1-59462-128-4*   **$29.95**
*The chief object of the following pages is to indicate some of the earliest ideas of mankind, as they are reflected in Ancient Law, and to point out the relation of those ideas to modern thought.*   Religiom/History Pages 452

**Far-Away Stories** *by William J. Locke*   ISBN: *1-59462-129-2*   **$19.45**
*"Good wine needs no bush, but a collection of mixed vintages does. And this book is just such a collection. Some of the stories I do not want to remain buried for ever in the museum files of dead magazine-numbers an author's not unpardonable vanity..."*   Fiction Pages 272

**Life of David Crockett** *by David Crockett*   ISBN: *1-59462-250-7*   **$27.45**
*"Colonel David Crockett was one of the most remarkable men of the times in which he lived. Born in humble life, but gifted with a strong will, an indomitable courage, and unremitting perseverance...*   Biographies/New Age Pages 424

**Lip-Reading** *by Edward Nitchie*   ISBN: *1-59462-206-X*   **$25.95**
*Edward B. Nitchie, founder of the New York School for the Hard of Hearing, now the Nitchie School of Lip-Reading, Inc, wrote "LIP-READING Principles and Practice". The development and perfecting of this meritorious work on lip-reading was an undertaking...*   How-to Pages 400

**A Handbook of Suggestive Therapeutics, Applied Hypnotism, Psychic Science**   ISBN: *1-59462-214-0*   **$24.95**
*by Henry Munro*
Health/New Age/Health/Self-help Pages 376

**A Doll's House: and Two Other Plays** *by Henrik Ibsen*   ISBN: *1-59462-112-8*   **$19.95**
*Henrik Ibsen created this classic when in revolutionary 1848 Rome. Introducing some striking concepts in playwriting for the realist genre, this play has been studied the world over.*   Fiction/Classics/Plays 308

**The Light of Asia** *by sir Edwin Arnold*   ISBN: *1-59462-204-3*   **$13.95**
*In this poetic masterpiece, Edwin Arnold describes the life and teachings of Buddha. The man who was to become known as Buddha to the world was born as Prince Gautama of India but he rejected the worldly riches and abandoned the reigns of power when...*   Religion/History/Biographies Pages 170

**The Complete Works of Guy de Maupassant** *by Guy de Maupassant*   ISBN: *1-59462-157-8*   **$16.95**
*"For days and days, nights and nights, I had dreamed of that first kiss which was to consecrate our engagement, and I knew not on what spot I should put my lips..."*   Fiction/Classics Pages 240

**The Art of Cross-Examination** *by Francis L. Wellman*   ISBN: *1-59462-309-0*   **$26.95**
*Written by a renowned trial lawyer, Wellman imparts his experience and uses case studies to explain how to use psychology to extract desired information through questioning.*   How-to/Science/Reference Pages 408

**Answered or Unanswered?** *by Louisa Vaughan*   ISBN: *1-59462-248-5*   **$10.95**
*Miracles of Faith in China*
Religion Pages 112

**The Edinburgh Lectures on Mental Science (1909)** *by Thomas*   ISBN: *1-59462-008-3*   **$11.95**
*This book contains the substance of a course of lectures recently given by the writer in the Queen Street Hall, Edinburgh. Its purpose is to indicate the Natural Principles governing the relation between Mental Action and Material Conditions...*   New Age/Psychology Pages 148

**Ayesha** *by H. Rider Haggard*   ISBN: *1-59462-301-5*   **$24.95**
*Verily and indeed it is the unexpected that happens! Probably if there was one person upon the earth from whom the Editor of this, and of a certain previous history, did not expect to hear again...*   Classics Pages 380

**Ayala's Angel** *by Anthony Trollope*   ISBN: *1-59462-352-X*   **$29.95**
*The two girls were both pretty, but Lucy who was twenty-one who supposed to be simple and comparatively unattractive, whereas Ayala was credited, as her Bombwhat romantic name might show, with poetic charm and a taste for romance. Ayala when her father died was nineteen...*   Fiction Pages 484

**The American Commonwealth** *by James Bryce*   ISBN: *1-59462-286-8*   **$34.45**
*An interpretation of American democratic political theory. It examines political mechanics and society from the perspective of Scotsman James Bryce*
Politics Pages 572

**Stories of the Pilgrims** *by Margaret P. Pumphrey*   ISBN: *1-59462-116-0*   **$17.95**
*This book explores pilgrims religious oppression in England as well as their escape to Holland and eventual crossing to America on the Mayflower, and their early days in New England...*   History Pages 268

www.bookjungle.com *email: sales@bookjungle.com fax: 630-214-0564 mail: Book Jungle PO Box 2226 Champaign, IL 61825*

**QTY**

**The Fasting Cure** *by Sinclair Upton*　　　　　　　　　　ISBN: *1-59462-222-1*　**$13.95**
*In the Cosmopolitan Magazine for May, 1910, and in the Contemporary Review (London) for April, 1910, I published an article dealing with my experiences in fasting. I have written a great many magazine articles, but never one which attracted so much attention... New Age/Self Help/Health Pages 164*

**Hebrew Astrology** *by Sepharial*　　　　　　　　　　　ISBN: *1-59462-308-2*　**$13.45**
*In these days of advanced thinking it is a matter of common observation that we have left many of the old landmarks behind and that we are now pressing forward to greater heights and to a wider horizon than that which represented the mind-content of our progenitors...　Astrology Pages 144*

**Thought Vibration or The Law of Attraction in the Thought World**　ISBN: *1-59462-127-6*　**$12.95**

*by William Walker Atkinson*　　　　　　　　　　　　　　　*Psychology/Religion Pages 144*

**Optimism** *by Helen Keller*　　　　　　　　　　　　　ISBN: *1-59462-108-X*　**$15.95**
*Helen Keller was blind, deaf, and mute since 19 months old, yet famously learned how to overcome these handicaps, communicate with the world, and spread her lectures promoting optimism. An inspiring read for everyone...　Biographies/Inspirational Pages 84*

**Sara Crewe** *by Frances Burnett*　　　　　　　　　　　ISBN: *1-59462-360-0*　**$9.45**
*In the first place, Miss Minchin lived in London. Her home was a large, dull, tall one, in a large, dull square, where all the houses were alike, and all the sparrows were alike, and where all the door-knockers made the same heavy sound...　Childrens/Classic Pages 88*

**The Autobiography of Benjamin Franklin** *by Benjamin Franklin*　ISBN: *1-59462-135-7*　**$24.95**
*The Autobiography of Benjamin Franklin has probably been more extensively read than any other American historical work, and no other book of its kind has had such ups and downs of fortune. Franklin lived for many years in England, where he was agent...　Biographies/History Pages 332*

| Name | |
| --- | --- |
| Email | |
| Telephone | |
| Address | |
| | |
| City, State ZIP | |

☐ **Credit Card**　　　☐ **Check / Money Order**

| Credit Card Number | |
| --- | --- |
| Expiration Date | |
| Signature | |

Please Mail to:　Book Jungle
　　　　　　　　PO Box 2226
　　　　　　　　Champaign, IL 61825
　　or Fax to:　　630-214-0564

## ORDERING INFORMATION

**web**: *www.bookjungle.com*
**email**: *sales@bookjungle.com*
**fax**: *630-214-0564*
**mail**: *Book Jungle  PO Box 2226  Champaign, IL 61825*
**or PayPal** *to sales@bookjungle.com*

*Please contact us for bulk discounts*

## DIRECT-ORDER TERMS

**20% Discount if You Order
Two or More Books**
Free Domestic Shipping!
Accepted: Master Card, Visa,
Discover, American Express